CROWNED FOR THE SHEIKH'S BABY

CROWNED FOR THE SHEIKH'S BABY

SHARON KENDRICK

MILLS & BOON

First published in Great Britain 2018
by Mills & Boon, an imprint of HarperCollins*Publishers*
1 London Bridge Street, London, SE1 9GF

Large Print edition 2018

ISBN: 978-0-263-07430-7

MIX
Paper from responsible sources
FSC C007454

This book is produced from independently certified FSC™ paper to ensure responsible forest management. For more information visit www.harpercollins.co.uk/green.

Printed and bound in Great Britain
by CPI Group (UK) Ltd, Croydon, CR0 4YY

This book is dedicated to the urbane and dashingly handsome Matt Newman, with thanks and gratitude for his generous donation to the amazing charity The Back-Up Trust.

PROLOGUE

We trust you will find everything to your satisfaction.

KULAL'S MOUTH HARDENED into a cynical smile. As if. When did anything in life ever *truly* satisfy?

Crushing the handwritten note—one of the many personal touches which made this Sardinian hotel complex so achingly luxurious—he threw it into the bin in a perfect arcing shot and walked over to the balcony.

Restlessly, his eyes skated over the horizon. He wondered why he could feel no joy in his heart or why the warmth of the sun left him feeling cold. He had just achieved a life's ambition by bringing together some of the world's biggest oil moguls. They'd told him it was impossible. That masterminding the diaries of so many powerful men simply couldn't be done. But Kulal had proved them wrong. He liked proving people wrong, just as he enjoyed defying the expectations which had been heaped on him since the day his older brother had turned his back on his heritage and left him to rule.

He had worked day and night to make this conference happen. To convince attendees with his famously seductive tongue that it was time to look at renewable energy sources, rather than relying on the fossil fuels of old. Kings and sheikhs had agreed with him and pledges had been made. The cheers following his opening speech had echoed long into the night. There were now but a few days left for him to hammer out the fine details of the deal—and he was able to do it in a place which many people considered close to paradise. Yet he felt…

He gave a heavy sigh which mingled with the warm Sardinian breeze.

Certainly not drunk with glory, as other men in his position might be, and he couldn't work out why. At thirty-four, he was considered by many to be at his intellectual and physical peak. He was known as a fair, if sometimes autocratic ruler and he ruled a prosperous land. And yes, he had a few enemies at court—men who would have preferred his twin brother to have been King because they considered him more malleable. But all rulers had to deal with insurrection. It came with the job—it was certainly nothing *new*.

So why wasn't he punching the air with glee? Kulal contemplated the horizon without really seeing it. Perhaps he had been working so hard that he'd neglected the more basic needs of his body. Not to put too fine a point on it—his legendary libido, which had been sidelined ever since he had finished with his long-term mistress a few months back. It didn't help that she had made the break-up official with a tearful interview in one of those glossy magazines that filled women's heads with meaningless froth. And that as a consequence, his name had zoomed back to the top of one of those tedious 'most eligible' lists—and he now seemed to be on some kind of matrimonial hit list. Rather ironic since he had always avoided marriage like the plague, no matter how determined the woman.

He yawned. His relationship with the international supermodel had lasted almost a year—a record for him. He had chosen her not just because she was blonde and leggy and could work wonders with her tongue, but because she seemed to accept what he would and wouldn't tolerate in a relationship. But in the end, she had sabotaged it with her neediness. He'd stated at the start that he wouldn't put a ring on her finger. That he had no desire for family or long-term commitment. Because didn't domesticity forge cold chains, which could suffocate? He had promised sex, diamonds and a fancy apartment—and had honoured those pledges in full. But she had wanted more. Women always did. They wanted to bleed you dry until there was nothing left.

Dark and bitter memories washed over him, but he forced himself to block them out as he leaned against the rail of the balcony, looking out at boats bobbing around on the Mediterranean. He thought how different this busy stretch of water was from the peace of the Murjaan Sea, which lapped on the eastern shores of his desert homeland. But then, everything about this place was different. The sights. The scents. The sounds. The women who lay on sun-loungers in their minuscule bikinis. One of his aides had told him that the loungers directly beneath his penthouse suite were always the first to go—presumably occupied by those hoping to catch the eye of Zahristan's Desert King. Kulal's lips curved in disdain. Did they, like so many others, imagine themselves in the role of Queen? That they would succeed where so many had failed?

Surveying the women directly beneath him, he felt not a flicker of excitement as he glanced at their half-naked bodies, which glistened in the sun. He thought they looked like oiled pieces of chicken about to be thrown onto the barbecue, their half-open mouths thick with lipstick and tilted straw hats protecting their hair extensions.

And then he saw her.

Kulal tensed, his eyes narrowing and his heart beginning to pound.

Did she capture his focus and keep it captured because she was wearing more than anyone else, as she hurried across the terrace with an anxious look on her face? In fact, she was wearing the standard hotel uniform—a plain yellow dress, which was straining over her voluminous breasts and clinging to the swell of her curvy buttocks. He though how *fresh* she looked with that shiny ponytail swishing against her back as she walked. Certainly, when contrasted with all the flesh on show, the brunette seemed positively *wholesome* and, although such women were rare in Kulal's world, he reminded himself that she was a member of the hotel staff. And sleeping with staff was never a good idea.

But a small sigh escaped his lips as he turned away.

Pity.

CHAPTER ONE

'HANNAH, DO NOT look so nervous. I merely said I wished to speak to you about the Sheikh.'

Hannah tried to smile as she looked up at Madame Martin—fixing her face into the kind of expression which would be expected of a highly experienced chambermaid. She must look eager—and at all times, because this job was the opportunity of a lifetime and breaks like this didn't come along very often. Wasn't it true that every other chambermaid at the Granchester in London had been green with envy when Hannah had been picked to work in the fancy Sardinian branch of the hotel group because they were short-staffed? She suspected they would have been even more envious if they'd realised that Sheikh Kulal Al Diya was a guest here—a billionaire desert king who everyone on this Mediterranean island seemed to think was some kind of walking sex god.

But not her.

No, definitely not her. She'd only seen him a couple of times, but each time he'd terrified her with all that dark brooding stuff going on and that way he had of slanting his black eyes in a way which had made her feel most peculiar. Hadn't her breasts sprung into alarming life the first time she'd seen him, causing her nipples to feel as if they were about to burst right through her bra? And hadn't she wanted to squirm with a strange and unfamiliar hunger as that ebony gaze had swept over her? For once, she hadn't felt in control and that had made her feel extremely uncomfortable, because Hannah liked to feel in control.

She brushed her clammy palms down over her lemon-coloured uniform—a bad idea since it drew the attention of Madame Martin to her hips and instantly the Frenchwoman frowned.

'Tiens!' she exclaimed. 'Your dress is a little tight, *n'est ce pas*?'

'It's the only one they had which fitted, Madame Martin,' said Hannah apologetically.

The elegant woman who was in charge of all the domestic staff at Hotel L'Idylle raised her perfectly plucked eyebrows. *'C'est vrai.'* She gave a resigned sigh. 'You Englishwomen are… 'Ow you say? Big girls!'

Hannah's smile didn't slip because who was she to deny the truth behind Madame Martin's words? She certainly wasn't as slim as her continental peers. She liked her food, had a healthy appetite and wasn't going to make any apology for it. Like much else, mealtimes had been unpredictable when she'd been growing up and you never forgot something like that. She'd never forget the dull gnaw of hunger, or how eagerly she'd seized on any scraps she'd managed to salvage to put together something resembling a meal. She didn't spend her life picking at her food, that was for sure—unlike her sister, who seemed to think that eating was an unnecessary waste of time.

But she wasn't going to worry about her sister, or dwell on the troubled times of their growing-up years. Hadn't that been one of the reasons for leaping on this job so eagerly—even though she'd never even been out of England before? She had decided she was going to start living her life differently from now on and the first part of that plan was to stop worrying about her baby sister. Because Tamsyn wasn't a baby any more; she was only two years younger and perfectly able to stand on her own two feet—except that was never going to happen if Hannah kept bailing her out every time she got herself into trouble.

So think about yourself for once, she reminded herself—and concentrate on the unbelievable bonus you've been offered for a few months of working in this Sardinian paradise.

'What exactly did you wish to talk to me about, Madame Martin?' she enquired eagerly.

The Frenchwoman smiled. 'You are very good at your job, Hannah. It is why you were sent here by our London branch, but I have observed you myself and thoroughly approve of their choice. The way you fold a bedsheet is a joy to watch.'

Hannah inclined her head to accept the compliment. 'Thank you.'

'You are quiet and unobtrusive. You move *comme une souris*—like a mouse,' Madame Martin translated in reply to Hannah's confused look. 'Put it this way—nobody would ever notice you in a room.'

'Thank you,' said Hannah again, rather more cautiously this time because she wasn't sure if that really sounded like a compliment.

'Which is why the management have decided to give you some extra responsibility.'

Hannah nodded, because this was something she was good at. Throw responsibility at her and she would soak it up like a sponge with water. 'Yes, *madame*?' she said and waited.

'What do you know about Sheikh Kulal Al Diya?'

Hannah tried to smile, but it was difficult when an unwanted shiver was rippling its way down her spine. 'He is the ruler of Zahristan, one of the biggest oil-producing countries in the world, but he's a leading exponent of alternative energy.

All the staff were briefed about him before he arrived,' she added hastily, in response to Madame Martin's look of surprise.

'Bien,' said the Frenchwoman approvingly. 'It was he who organised this international meeting, which has brought so many prestigious leaders to the hotel and has done much to elevate the profile of our new conference centre.'

'Yes, Madame Martin,' said Hannah, still not quite sure where this was heading.

'And you are perhaps aware that many people have been trying to seek out the Sheikh's company,' said Madame Martin slowly. 'Since he is a man of great influence.'

'I'm sure they do.' Hannah noted the pause which followed and which she somehow got the idea she was expected to fill. 'It was exactly the same in the London branch of the Granchester—the more powerful the guest, the more people want to get to know them.'

'Especially if the man happens to be newly single and extremely good-looking,' said Madame Martin, with a busy wiggle of her manicured fingers. 'But His Royal Highness has no wish to be the focus of the attentions which someone in his position always attracts. It is why he occasionally chooses to travel with only a very modest entourage, but unfortunately that only makes him more accessible to the general public. Why, only last night, a well-known heiress managed to bribe her way past security and make her way to his table.'

Hannah winced. 'Was there a scene, *madame*?'

'I'm afraid there was, and we do not tolerate "scenes" here at L'Idylle. Which is why, for the remainder of his stay, Sheikh Al Diya intends to finish the rest of his business in the sanctuary of his suite, which is certainly big enough to accommodate his needs.' There was a pause. 'And why you are being assigned to work exclusively for him.'

Hannah screwed up her face in confusion. 'You mean, I'm to make his bed and change his towels?'

'Of course. But you will also serve His Royal Highness any meals he orders and make sure there are drinks and snacks for his guests. Keep the water in the flowers topped up. Tidy up after him and make sure that nobody unauthorised tries to gain entry to his rooms. Security here is tight, but there is no such thing as completely reliable security. Why, even in your famous Buckingham Palace, intruders have successfully gained access, is that not so?' The Frenchwoman's face grew stern. 'Do you think you are capable of what I am asking of you, Hannah?'

Hannah's first instinct was to say no. To protest that she was a chambermaid and nothing more. Someone who silently serviced the hotel bedrooms and learnt more about the guests than they would probably be comfortable with, if they only realised how many clues about themselves they left laying around the place. She wasn't really confident enough to wait on a desert king, or to swish around topping up the water in expensive vases of flowers. She wasn't really a *maid.*

'Isn't there someone else who would rather do it, Madame Martin?' she questioned doubtfully. 'Someone with a bit more experience of that kind of thing?'

'Indeed there is.' Madame Martin pursed her lips. 'I am sure I could have the female staff queuing from here to our capital city of Cagliari, but none of them have your characteristics, Hannah. You are a young woman whose head is planted firmly on her shoulders, as you English say. You will not be seduced by a pair of flashing black eyes and a body which makes grown women shiver.' Madame Martin seemed suddenly to realise what she was saying, and as she pulled herself together, she fixed Hannah with another stern look. 'Can I rely on you to accept this task, so that I can report back favourably to your superiors in London?'

Hannah swallowed as she recognised it was going to be impossible to refuse—and why would anyone in their right mind want to? Surely a temporary promotion was a good thing. A chance to get the pay-rise she'd been hoping for. A pay-rise which might make it possible for her to one day buy a tiny place of her own.

A home of her own.

The chance to put down roots at last.

'Will you do that, my dear?' prompted the Frenchwoman kindly.

Hannah swallowed down the sudden lump which seemed to be clogging up her throat, wondering why she still reacted so stupidly to someone speaking to her with affection.

Because she wasn't used to it?

Or because she mistrusted it?

Nodding her head, she produced a tentative smile. 'I would be honoured, Madame Martin,' she said.

'Bien.' Madame Martin gave a brisk nod. 'Then come with me and I will show you around the suite of His Royal Highness.'

Hannah followed her superior along wide and airy corridors, which overlooked the small, natural harbour outside. Purple bougainvillea rippled softly in the breeze and the sky was the bluest she had ever seen. Every day was the same—picture-book perfect. Or at least, that was how it seemed. It hadn't rained in paradise for as long as she'd been there and sometimes she could hardly believe she was.

Who would have thought it? Humble Hannah Wilson experiencing life in one of the fanciest resorts in Europe. The rootless orphan who'd never really known anything except making do was now working in a hotel which redefined the word luxury. A place which regularly entertained princes and tycoons, heiresses and film stars. And now a sheikh.

A sheikh for whom she was to work exclusively!

'You must continue to be unobtrusive,' Madame Martin was saying. 'When the Sheikh arrives in his suite, you will quietly enquire what he requires and make sure he gets it. Immediately.'

'And if he doesn't actually want…*anything*?' Hannah questioned cautiously.

'Then you will vacate the premises as quickly as possible and await further instruction. You are being moved to a small staff room just along the corridor from his suite. Can I rely on you, Hannah?'

Hannah nodded in agreement because what else could she do? 'Yes, Madame Martin.'

'One last thing.' The Frenchwoman's voice lowered into a conspiratorial whisper. 'The Sheikh is known as a man of great, shall we say—*appetite*.'

'You mean he likes his food?' questioned Hannah cautiously.

'No, I do not mean that.' An impatient shake of her head barely displaced an immaculate strand of Madame Martin's hair. 'I mean that he may have female guests visiting him and, should you find yourself dealing with them, you will treat them as if they were princesses. Which is probably their ambition,' she finished, with a dry laugh. 'Is that clear, Hannah?'

'Yes, *madame*,' answered Hannah as they entered the elevator, slotting in the special card which gave access to the exclusive penthouse suite, a journey which took mere seconds before the doors slid open. Hannah saw two bulky men in dark suits standing poker-faced on either side of a large door and she blinked. Could those bulges she could see in their pockets possibly be *guns*? She guessed they could. Of *course* the Sheikh would have bodyguards who looked as if they were made of steel and iron, rather than flesh and blood. Whose eyes didn't even flicker as she stared up at them. A sudden realisation of what she had let herself in for made her spine tingle with apprehension.

'*Voilà!* We are here,' said Madame Martin. 'Come.'

After a cursory knock, which went unanswered, the door was unlocked and Madame Martin walked straight in. Hannah thought she was prepared for any eventuality…for dancing girls, or some kind of harem. Or maybe a smoke-filled room where some kind of high-stakes card game was taking place.

What she had not been prepared for was the sight which greeted her—of the Sheikh himself. Her eyes nearly bulged out of their sockets and her throat dried to dust. After the kind of build-up she'd been given, Hannah wouldn't have been surprised to see him lying half-naked on one of the sumptuous velvet sofas, while some gorgeous nubile woman administered to him with warm oils. Or wearing something lavish and ceremonial—golden robes, perhaps—which swished as he walked.

In fact, he was seated at a desk which overlooked one of the resort's many swimming pools and there wasn't a golden robe in sight. He was wearing dark trousers and a blue shirt so pale that it was almost white. The shirt had two top buttons undone and the sleeves had been rolled up to reveal his hair-darkened forearms. Hannah noted these things almost automatically—perhaps as a kind of defensive mechanism. As if labelling the most commonplace things about him could protect her from the impact his sudden searing black gaze was having on her.

Because there was nothing commonplace about his face. It was a face in a million, no question about that. An unforgettable face—with those imperiously high cheekbones and his hair which gleamed like sunlit tar. The olive skin of his hawk-like features glowed with health and vitality, and there was an unmistakably arrogant tilt to his proud jaw. But it was the eyes which did it. She'd seen them from a distance, but up close they were unsettling. More than unsettling. Hannah swallowed. Hard and unflickering and blacker than any eyes had the right to be. And they were staring at her. Staring as if she had some smut on her nose, or the dark stain of sweat at her armpits. Hannah shifted uncomfortably beneath the intensity of that gaze, her hands nervously fluttering to brush away imagined dust from her slightly too small dress until she remembered that she wasn't supposed to be drawing attention to her hips like that.

'I am extremely sorry to disturb you, Sheikh Al Diya,' Madame Martin was saying smoothly. 'But since no one answered my knock, I assumed nobody was here.'

'I did not hear you knock otherwise I should have sent you away,' said the Sheikh, an impatient wave of his hand indicating the mountain of paperwork piled in front of him. 'As you see, I am busy.'

'Of course, Your Royal Highness. Perhaps you would prefer us to come back at a more suitable time?'

Kulal put his pen down and studied the two women who were standing before him—the too thin French matron and the curvy chambermaid he'd seen hurrying across the patio a couple of days earlier, with an anxious look on her face. What he would *prefer* was not to have been interrupted in the first place because he was at a very delicate stage of negotiation. But suddenly, the ever-engrossing topic of solar power melted away as he stared at the ponytailed brunette whose fingers were smoothing down her unsightly uniform dress.

Was that an unconscious gesture to draw his attention to the fecundity of her hips and breasts? he wondered. Or was it deliberate? Either way, she had hit the jackpot. No doubt she was aware that her ripe body was designed to send his hormones shooting into disarray and, inconveniently, they were doing just that. He felt his groin tightening as he imagined his tongue trailing a slow path over those magnificent breasts, and for a moment, he cursed the insidious power of Mother Nature—for were they not all puppets in her need to continue the human race? And *that* was the reason behind his instinct to get the chambermaid horizontal as quickly as possible, before impaling her with his hardness.

He expected her to meet his gaze with a knowing look of challenge, for he had never met a woman who wouldn't put out for him within the first minutes of meeting. But the humble chambermaid had dropped her gaze to the ground, her cheeks blooming like roses as she studied the Persian rug at her feet with a fierce intensity.

Unusual, conceded Kulal as he leaned back in his chair. Very unusual. 'Now that you have managed to successfully interrupt my train of thought,' he said acidly, 'you might as well tell me why you are here.'

'I was showing Hannah around your suite, Your Royal Highness.'

Hannah. Kulal ran a slow finger around the circumference of his mouth. An ordinary name yet somehow it pleased him.

'Because?' he interrogated.

'In view of the enormous interest your presence

has generated, and after the unfortunate scene in the main restaurant last night, we decided it would be preferable for you to have your own private maid for the duration of your stay,' said Madame Martin. 'Especially since His Royal Highness has brought with him only a skeleton staff.'

'Because I have no wish to burden myself with the cumbersome accruements of the royal court!' snapped Kulal. 'You try travelling with an entourage of a thousand and five hundred tons of luggage, like some of my desert neighbours! If I fill the entire hotel complex with my staff, then how the hell is there going to be room for anyone else?'

'Quite so. And I can only imagine your aversion to such a logistical nightmare, Your Royal Highness,' replied Madame Martin diplomatically. 'Which is why one of your aides made the request earlier and why we are assigning you Hannah, who from now on will be exclusively under your command.'

This was language Kulal was used to.

Command.

Exclusivity.

Words of possession and control, which went hand in hand with being a sheikh. But somehow the words had taken on an unexpectedly erotic flavour when applied to the curvy little servant who stood in front of him. He felt his heart miss a beat as he looked at her still-bent head, the straightness of her parting cutting a stark white line through her shiny brown hair. But her shoulders were stiff and if her body language was anything to go by, she certainly wasn't as honoured by her sudden promotion as perhaps she should have been. And despite the knowledge that fraternising with the staff was a very bad idea, Kulal couldn't deny that he found such an unusual response curiously *exciting*.

'So how do you feel about working for me, Hannah?' he questioned softly.

She looked up then and he was surprised by eyes of a startling hue—blue eyes which resembled the colour of the aquamarines his mother used to wear around her throat. Expensive jewels bought by his father in an attempt to compensate for his frequent absences. As if pieces of glass could ever compensate. But his mother had been weak. Weak and manipulative. Prepared to put her own desperate needs above those of her children. Kulal's mouth hardened as he obliterated the harsh memories and listened to the chambermaid's response.

'I am happy to serve you in any way I can, Your Royal Highness,' she said.

She delivered the words as if she had been coached and maybe she had, for they were dutiful rather than meaningful. A rare flicker of humour lifted Kulal's lips, but it was gone as quickly as it had arrived. He gave a dismissive nod and picked up his pen. 'Very well,' he said as he pulled one of the documents towards him. 'Just make sure you don't disturb me. Not in any way. Do you understand?'

'Yes, Your Royal Highness,' she said, still in that same dutiful voice, and Kulal found himself almost disappointed when she bobbed a clumsy kind of curtsey before backing out of the room as if she couldn't wait to get away from him.

CHAPTER TWO

DON'T DISTURB ME. That had been the Sheikh's only instruction when she'd first started working for him, but Hannah wondered how the powerful Kulal Al Diya would react if he knew how much he was disturbing *her.*

She wished he wouldn't look at her that way.

She wished he wouldn't make her *feel* this way.

Or was it all a figment of her imagination? Was his searing ebony gaze *really* lingering on her for longer than was necessary, or was that simply wishful thinking on her part? One thing she certainly wasn't imagining was the aching of her body in response to that look. Whenever he walked into the room, her senses felt as if they'd been brought to life—yet was she really misguided enough to think the sexy desert King would give a second glance at her—plain and inexperienced Hannah Wilson?

Her heart was pounding as she prepared his coffee. After his short-tempered response at their initial meeting she had expected him to be difficult to work for. She'd thought he would be all distant and haughty, as befitted a man of his status. Yet it was funny how sustained contact with someone could make them seem more human—even someone as exulted as a desert king.

She tipped extra sugar cubes into a porcelain bowl because the Sheikh was rather partial to sugar. In fact, as far as she could make out, sweetening his coffee was the closest he got to indulgence. He didn't drink alcohol, nor smoke those pungent cigars which some of the richer clients puffed on when they were out on the smoking terrace. He even seemed able to go without food for long periods of time—as if fasting came naturally to him. Which might explain the magnificence of his iron-hard body which she had once seen—inadvertently—when he had emerged unexpectedly from the shower.

Even now it made her breathless to remember it. Diamond droplets of water had glittered against his dark skin and Hannah had found herself mesmerised by endlessly muscular legs and narrow hips against which the white towel slung round them had looked woefully inadequate. For a moment, she had been completely flummoxed, unprepared for the sudden rush of heat which had made tiny beads of sweat appear on her heated brow.

'Oh!' she remembered exclaiming weakly, clutching onto her feather duster as if it were a life-raft, yet unable to drag her gaze away from his spectacular body.

To his credit, he had seemed as surprised to see her as she was him, a deep frown making his jet-black eyes appear even more laser-like in their intensity than usual. 'What the hell are you doing here?' he had demanded.

'I work here, Your Royal Highness.'

'You told me you'd finished for the day.'

Hannah had been so startled by the realisation that he'd actually been listening to her that she'd begun to recount the boringly domestic reason why she'd still been on the premises. 'I had,' she'd said quickly. 'Only I spotted a cobweb, high up on one of the ceilings, and since I thought you'd already left for your helicopter flight—'

'You decided to destroy the poor spider's home?' he'd drawled, his eyes gleaming with what had appeared to be mischief. 'My, my, what a heartless woman you can be, Hannah.'

And Hannah had blushed even more. She had gone the colour of a beetroot or one of those dark 'heritage' tomatoes which room service kept always sending up whenever the Sheikh asked for a salad. Because she wasn't used to being teased—and she certainly wasn't used to being teased by a half-naked man, with an implied level of intimacy which was completely outside her comfort zone. Maybe that was why she'd blurted out the first stupid thing which had come into her head and said it with a fierceness which had seemed to take him by surprise.

'I would *never* kill a spider. They have just as much right to be here as we do.'

There had been a pause. 'Then I must be careful what I accuse you of in the future,' had been the Sheikh's slow and thoughtful response.

Even now Hannah's cheeks went pink when she remembered it. Did he say things like that just to get a rise out of her? Sometimes she suspected he did—until she forced herself to remember the reality of her situation. As if someone like Kulal Al Diya would have the inclination to tease the lowliest of hotel workers when she knew for a fact that a famous American singer with an instantly recognisable name had called him yesterday afternoon. Hannah had almost dropped the phone when she'd answered it. Briefly, she'd thought about how much this particular woman's autograph would raise if you auctioned it on the Internet—before handing the phone over to the black-eyed desert King. The Sheikh had shut the door of his bedroom to take the call in private… and Hannah had been unprepared for the sudden rush of envy she had experienced.

And that was when she'd started wondering what it would be like to have a man like Kulal

Al Diya as your lover. Imagining what it would be like to wake up in those powerful arms while his black eyes raked over you. Or how it would feel to have those long fingers slowly stroking skin which was growing heated even as she thought about it.

Just *stop* it, Hannah. Had that cheesy film she'd watched on her day off kick-started such crazy fantasies? Or was it because she'd been sitting there with nothing but a bumper carton of popcorn for company, surrounded by couples who were making out? With an impatient click of her lips, Hannah straightened an embroidered silk cushion. For some people, this would have been the job from heaven but it was rapidly turning into the job from hell—and all because she couldn't stop obsessing about a hotel guest in a totally unprofessional way. Had she chosen someone completely out of reach because that was *safe*?

Or was it talking to her sister the other night which had made Hannah feel more of a loser in love than usual? Tamsyn had sent a photo of herself about to go out for the evening, her red hair cascading down her back like a fiery waterfall, her big green eyes fringed with spectacular black lashes. And hadn't Hannah felt a little *resentful*—wondering how it was that, despite Tamsyn's dire financial situation and lack of regular employment, she could still manage to look like a film star and go out and have a good time?

'Are you ever going to serve that coffee, Hannah? Or are you just going to stand there muttering to yourself all morning?'

The richly accented voice breaking into her thoughts made Hannah jump and she turned to see the Sheikh sauntering into the room, with all the unleashed power of a hand-reared leopard. She watched as he sat down. It had taken a bit of adjustment to get used to his western taste in clothing because she hadn't realised that sheikhs wore *jeans*...especially not spray-on faded ones which made him look like a poster star for the brand. Her fingers tightened around the coffee cup, but not nearly as much as her breasts were tightening beneath the snug fit of her uniform dress. *Had* she been talking out loud?

Was he aware she'd been having stupid fantasies about him?

Of course he wasn't—he might be a famously good negotiator, but he wasn't that clever!

'Certainly, Your Royal Highness,' she said efficiently as she carried the cup over to his desk, where he was looking at some exotic-looking map. He liked looking at maps, and on one memorable occasion had pointed out a mountain range on the north-eastern side of his country, describing the snowy peaks in a way which had made Hannah feel all dreamy. He'd told her about Mount Taljan, which was the highest and most beautiful mountain in all of Zahristan, casually mentioning that he'd scaled it when he was just seventeen years old.

He looked up as she put the cup down in front of him, his black eyes raking over her like glowing coals and, as usual, she was momentarily flustered by the intensity of that gaze.

'Is…is there anything else I can get you, Your Royal Highness?' she questioned politely.

Kulal leaned back in his chair to study her,

knowing if he did so for long enough then her cheeks would inevitably take on that rosy hue he found so entrancing. And then she would squirm with embarrassment until he put her out of her misery and dismissed her. His lips curved into a reflective smile. He knew she was attracted to him—which came as no great surprise; what *was* surprising was her total lack of attempt to capture his interest, especially given her rare proximity to his royal presence. In his own country, the majority of his personal servants were male and, in the west, few women would have been given the unfettered access which Hannah had been granted.

Yet there had been no change to her outward appearance, which would have been usual. No subtle lick of lipstick, or an application of mascara to make those extraordinary aquamarine eyes look even bigger. Nor copious amounts of perfume applied to wrist or cleavage, intended to beguile his nostrils with the scent of her femininity. His eyes narrowed. And wasn't her lack of artifice refreshing—coupled with a naivety which was rarely found in the world he inhabited?

He dropped a sugar cube into his coffee, and then a second before taking a sip. 'Excellent,' he murmured.

Hannah beamed with satisfaction. 'I trust everything else is to your satisfaction, Your Royal Highness?'

He glowered. 'Why do the staff here keep saying that same thing over and over again?'

She wriggled her shoulders a little awkwardly. 'It's the Granchester's promise, Your Royal Highness. They like us to reinforce the group's core message.'

'Well, I've got the *core message* loud and clear so don't bother saying it to me again, understand?'

She pursed her lips together. 'Yes, Your Royal Highness.'

Kulal took another sip of coffee. He'd been awake until the early hours, fine-tuning the announcement which he planned to make to the world very soon—a dramatic development about cheaper solar power, which would inevitably stir up envy among his competitors. His time here on Sardinia was almost over and tomorrow he would return to Zahristan and the inevitable affairs of state which had been piling up in his absence. But before that happened, there was the little matter of an invitation to a party on the other side of the island, a party he could have easily given a miss, were it not being thrown by one of his oldest friends.

He stifled a sigh because he was in no mood for entertainment and not just because he could do with a good night's sleep. Parties were predictable and tedious. The same boring small-talk and disingenuous asides. And the more elevated your status, the more predictable they became. He scowled, for his recent break-up would only exacerbate the rush to pair him off with someone new. People spent far too much time contemplating his marital status and it was none of their damned business. Sometimes he thought he should put the world straight by openly stating his intention to defer marriage for as long as possible, but why fuel speculation?

He thought about the women who would doubtless be in attendance because his friend Salvatore believed that a vacancy in a man's bed should be filled as quickly as possible. And Salvatore had connections to some of the most desirable women in the world. The kind of women most men drooled about, with their gym-honed bodies and diamonds which some adoring daddy had probably bestowed on them for their eighteenth birthday. Women who would slip him little pieces of paper with their cell phone number written above a line of kisses.

Kulal yawned, because the idea of being hit on was failing to heat his blood and he allowed his gaze to return to the chambermaid who was self-consciously straightening cushions. As she straightened up, her cheeks automatically flared when she noticed her gaze on him and he could not resist a slow smile. When was the last time he'd seen a woman *blush* like that?

'You don't say very much, do you?' he observed.

'My role here is to attend to your needs, Your Royal Highness, not to converse,' she said primly.

'You're English?'

She surveyed him with a suspicious blinking of her eyes. 'I am, Your Royal Highness.'

'So what brings you to Sardinia?'

She hesitated, as if she was surprised he was asking. She should be, he thought wryly—because he was pretty surprised himself.

'I usually work for the Granchester in London,' she explained falteringly. 'Which is one of the finest hotels—'

'Yes. There's no need for any more corporate-speak,' he said sardonically. 'I know the chain well. And the owner, as it happens.'

Her eyes widened. 'You know Zac Constantinides?' she questioned breathlessly.

'I do. I'm currently doing some business with his cousin—Xan. He was here at the conference earlier in the week. You didn't realise? No. You probably didn't. He likes to keep a low profile.' His mouth twisted into a wry smile. 'He's lucky he's able to.'

Hannah frowned. Xan Constantinides. The name rang a bell. Had her sister mentioned it, or had she imagined that? 'Yes, Your Royal Highness,' she said, which was her default answer when she couldn't think of anything else to say.

'Continue with your story,' he instructed. 'About how you came to be working here.'

Hannah hesitated, because she didn't realise she was actually telling him a *story*. And why was he so interested in *her* all of a sudden? Was he planning to make a complaint—telling Madame Martin she'd been muttering to herself and flinging her duster at imaginary cobwebs? Or that she'd been stalking him, hanging around the place when she was supposed to have gone home in order to see him emerging half-naked from the shower? Hannah bit back a smile. No. Nobody would believe *that*. She strongly suspected that another reason why she'd been chosen for this job was because she was exactly the kind of person who *wouldn't* ogle the royal guest, despite the fact that nobody could deny his drop-dead gorgeousness.

She realised he was still fixing her with that carelessly questioning look and so she shrugged.

'They've been short-staffed here,' she explained. 'I'm not quite sure why. They needed someone to fly out here and join the chambermaid staff, and I was the one they picked.'

'Because?'

She shrugged. 'I suppose because I'm considered very reliable.'

His mouth curved into a smile. 'Reliable?'

'That's right.'

'You don't sound too happy about it.'

Hannah never knew what made her come out with it. What made her blurt out the truth to *him*, of all people—but she did. 'I'm not,' she admitted, with a slight rush of heat. 'Especially as I'm also known as steady and sensible.' She thought about the things people always said about her.

'Good old Hannah.'

'You want someone to fill in on New Year's Eve? Ask Hannah. She'll have nothing better to do.'

'But surely these are positive things?' the Sheikh was saying.

'I'm sure they are,' she answered stiffly. 'But they're not really what someone my age wants to be known for, are they? They're the sort of traits which are better suited to a woman of middle age.'

'And how old are you, Hannah?' Kulal questioned kindly, finding himself suddenly engrossed in the kind of conversation he could never remember having before.

She lowered her lashes to shade her magnificent eyes. 'Twenty-five.'

Twenty-five.

He had thought she was older. Or younger. Actually, when he stopped to think about it—and why would he have done that until a few moments ago?—she was of an indeterminate age. Her plain uniform dress was timeless and the high ponytail was like a flashback to those nineteen-fifties rock 'n' roll films one of his tutors had once smuggled into the palace before being sacked for his libertarian attitude. It was only after the tutor had left that Kulal had realised how much he had protected him and his twin brother against the realities of life in the royal residence—and once he had gone, how the scales had fallen from their eyes. Suddenly, there had been no filter between them and their warring parents, who had turned the gleaming citadel of the palace into a gilded battlefield.

Was that why Kulal was overcome by a feeling of benevolence towards this humble soul, who stood before him? By a sudden curiosity to see what the chambermaid looked like as a real woman, rather than a drab servant who was old before her time? She had spoken with a certain resignation—as if her life up until then had been short of fun, and something about the submissive set of her shoulders told him his assessment was probably accurate. Kulal had never experienced poverty, but his powers of observation had been well honed and he noticed that her ugly black shoes—although carefully polished—were decidedly thin and worn.

So couldn't he show her a little kindness? Wave a magic wand and introduce some glamour into her life? What if he took her as his guest to Salvatore's party? His eyes narrowed in silent calculation. Such an action would ward off the attentions of hungry women who might have heard he was single again. And wouldn't having a woman by his side free him up from having to spend any longer there than necessary? It wasn't as if his intentions towards the chambermaid were questionable—and not just because she was a member of staff. Because he knew what women were like. He was soon to leave the island and the last thing he needed was her plaintive sobs because he had bedded her and she'd fallen 'in love' with him. He gave a silent nod of satisfaction. He was being benevolent, nothing more—and there was no doubt that the mischievous subterfuge of his proposal would add a certain *spice* to the party.

'Are you busy tomorrow night?' he questioned slowly.

Quickly, she looked up. 'You mean, am I on duty? No, not officially, but if there's something special you need me to do—it will be very welcome overtime, Your Royal Highness. I'll just fill it in on my timesheet and submit it to Madame Martin.'

For a moment Kulal was irritated. So she thought

of spending extra time with him in terms of the overtime, did she? Didn't she realise the great honour he was about to offer her? It was an outrageous response yet, curiously, it spurred him on and not simply because he'd never been side-lined in such a way before. Because surely a young woman of twenty-five should be thinking about more than her *salary*—especially when she was living on this stunning Mediterranean island. Idly he wondered if she had ever worn silk next to that creamy skin which blushed so easily, or whether she had ever danced beneath the stars. Wasn't it about time she did?

'I'd like you to come to a party with me,' he said.

Her face assumed a wary expression. 'You mean, to work?'

'No, not to work,' he negated, a flick of his hand indicating his impatience. 'As my guest.'

Her head jerked back. 'Your guest?'

'That's right.'

Unvarnished nails on show, she splayed her fingers over her breastbone and let out an odd kind of squeak. *'Me?'*

'Why not?' he drawled. 'You don't strike me as someone who goes to many parties and I thought that all women liked parties, and the chance to dress up. Wouldn't it be fun to do something different for a change?'

'You're inviting me to a party because you feel sorry for me?' she said in a small voice.

'Partially, yes,' he agreed, surprised enough by the honesty of her question to give her an equally honest reply. 'But your presence at my side will be advantageous to me.'

She screwed up her face. 'I'm not sure why.'

'It will deter other women from hitting on me. Because I'm not in the mood for predatory.' His eyes glittered. 'Frankly, I am bored with predatory.'

Her cheeks went very pink when he said that and she shifted awkwardly from one flat and clumpy black shoe to the other before shaking her head. 'It's very kind of you to ask me, Your Royal Highness, but I'm afraid I can't do it.'

'Can't?' Kulal frowned, because hesitation was one thing but refusal was something else. Something he wasn't used to and would not tolerate. 'Why not?'

'Because members of staff aren't allowed to fraternise with the guests. It's a hotel rule and grounds for instant dismissal.'

His smile grew wolfish. 'Only if they get to know about it.'

'Everyone will know about it!'

'How? This is a very exclusive party and it's on the other side of the island. I doubt whether anyone else from the hotel will even be invited and even if they are, they aren't going to recognise you.'

Again that suspicious look. 'Why not?'

Kulal slanted her a smile, her genuine reluctance fuelling his determination. 'Because you won't be in uniform.'

She stared at him uncomprehendingly.

'Wouldn't you like to put on something pretty for a change?' he continued. 'To dress like a princess, even if it's only for one night?'

'I don't have anything remotely princess-like in my wardrobe,' she said woodenly.

'Then let me fix it so that you do.'

Again, those aquamarine eyes narrowed with suspicion rather than the gratitude he would have expected.

'How would you do that?'

'Easy.' Kulal shrugged. 'All I have to do is pick up the phone and have one of my staff find you someone who deals with such matters. Someone discreet who can transform you into someone even you won't recognise.'

'You mean like Cinderella?' she said slowly.

His lips curved, for his tutor had also taught him about the English obsession with fairy tales and their need to transpose them onto real life. 'If you like.'

She tilted her chin upwards and, for the first time, he saw a flash of spirit in her aquamarine eyes. 'Does that mean my clothes will turn back into rags at midnight?'

'You can keep the dress, if that's what you're angling for.'

'I wasn't!' she said, before shaking her head. 'Look, it's very nice of you to offer but it's…it's a crazy idea and I can't do it. It's too risky.'

'Haven't you ever taken a risk, Hannah?' he questioned softly. 'Haven't you ever done something you shouldn't?'

And *that* was what got to Hannah—the definite challenge in his voice, which was laced with slight contempt. She looked into the gleam of his hard eyes and thought about it. Of *course* she'd never done anything dangerous, because keeping to the straight and narrow had been the only way she and her sister had been able to survive. And that way of living had stuck to her like glue. She'd got the first job she'd applied for and kept her head down. She'd been cautious and careful and saved what little money she could and used her leisure time trying to make up for her woeful lack of education by studying.

Just as she kept fit by taking scenic hikes through the English countryside, which were beautiful as well as free. But she'd never done anything impetuous or stepped outside her comfort zone, and maybe it was starting to show. Was her attitude making her old before her time? Was that why she was considered a no-risk temptation for the sexy Sheikh? Frumpy Hannah Wilson who would one day look in the mirror and discover she'd become the lonely middle-aged woman she'd been channelling all these years.

She met the desert King's mocking gaze, trying to ignore the sudden thrill of possibility which had started bubbling up inside her. Trying to dampen it down with her habitual sensible attitude, but suddenly the temptation was too strong for her to resist and she licked her lips.

Could she do it?

Should she do it?

And then she looked at him and her heart gave a dangerous leap. How could he manage to look so *edgy* even when he was doing something as benign as sitting in a chair, drinking coffee? With his black eyes and faintly mocking smile, he was the most gorgeous man she'd ever set eyes on and nobody like him was ever likely to make such a proposition to her again. So what if she *was* just there to protect him from predatory women, or if he was insisting on giving her some kind of makeover in case she disgraced him? Wouldn't this be something to tell the grandchildren, if she ever found a man she wanted to marry and vice versa? Something to mention casually to Tamsyn next time her sister nagged her about leading such a boring life?

'Very well, I'll do it,' she said, and, because he seemed to be waiting for something else, she stumbled out her thanks. 'Th-thank you very much indeed, Your Royal Highness.'

'You're welcome,' he drawled, eyes gleaming. 'But if you're going to do a convincing impression of being my date, you're going to have to stop using my title—especially in that deferential way. Call me Kulal. Try to talk to me as if I was a normal date.'

As colour flooded into her cheeks Hannah wondered what he'd say if he knew she wasn't really the kind of person who had normal dates. Nor any kind of date, really. 'I'll try.'

'Go on, then. Say my name.'

He was gazing at her expectantly and Hannah found herself complying. 'Kulal…' she whispered, thinking how strange it felt to use his first name. More than strange. Just the sound of it coming from her lips felt…*sexy*.

'Very good,' he said, and smiled. 'That wasn't *too* difficult, was it?'

A look of complicity flowed from his black eyes and Hannah was aware that, with that simple exchange, something had been forged between them. A secret which separated them from the rest of the world. Wasn't that called *collusion*?

The enormity of what she was about to do washed over her. 'Nobody must…' She looked at him and swallowed.

He raised his dark brows. 'Nobody must what, Hannah?' he prompted silkily.

'Nobody must find out,' she finished quickly. 'Or I'll lose my job.'

CHAPTER THREE

AT A RARE loss for words, Kulal stared at the woman who stood before him.

The little chambermaid...transformed!

He studied her for a long moment and felt a flicker of apprehension whisper over his skin. Would he so willingly have offered to have a stylist dress her if he'd realised that the end result was going to be quite so...*tantalising*? That the bodice of her silk dress would cling so entrancingly to her breasts—emphasising their lush weight in a way which the lemon uniform had only hinted at?

He swallowed. The long, floaty dress outlined her shapely legs and gave a glimpse of the bare toes which peeped from glittering sandals as she walked towards him. The functional ponytail was now a distant memory, and her hair tumbled in a dark and silky profusion around her shoulders and, dazedly, Kulal shook his head. Had he been completely naïve? he wondered impatiently. Had he played Pygmalion by bringing the curvy little statue to life, without even stopping to consider that her resulting sensuality was something he would now have to spend the rest of the evening resisting? Had he *really* thought he would be nothing but a cool onlooker, curiously observing the results of her expensive makeover? *Yes, he had.* He said something low and fervent in his native tongue and immediately she fixed him with a look of uncertainty.

'You don't like it?' she said tentatively.

He didn't quite trust himself to reply immediately. Instead, he turned the question round. 'Do you?'

She shrugged and the movement drew his attention to the creamy swell of her breasts—as if any extra encouragement were needed!

'I'm not sure,' she said, her hands skating over the wide beam of her hips against which floated layers of ice-blue silk. 'You don't think it's too much?'

'Too much for what?' he questioned roughly. 'You certainly won't be overdressed, if that's what you're worried about.'

It wasn't. Hannah swayed a little on her sky-scraper sandals. Her main worry was that she wouldn't be able to live up to the image of what these clothes represented. Because she'd stared into the mirror and seen someone she didn't recognise staring back. A polished woman exuding a sophistication which was fake. She felt like a fraud—which was exactly what she was. A hotel employee dressed up to look like one of the guests. What if someone started talking to her and realised that she hadn't got much to say for herself—and that all the glossy potential of her appearance was false? What if someone sussed her out and *reported* her?

'I'm worried how we're going to get out of the hotel without me being noticed.'

He smiled suddenly as if he had decided to enjoy the subterfuge. 'Oh, don't worry about that,' he said airily. 'It's all taken care of.'

Hannah soon realised that Kulal wasn't exaggerating—and that pretty much anything was possible when you were a king. He might not have a full entourage of staff in tow, but there were enough bodyguards and heavies who seemed to appear from out of nowhere to swarm around them in a protective coterie as they were taken through the maze of back corridors to the helipad outside where a helicopter was waiting. And even if anyone *had* bothered to spare Hannah a second glance—most eyes were on the imperious strut of the Sheikh, because he was the one who commanded everyone's attention. Nobody would have guessed that the woman in the expensive dress and glittering jewels was really a humble chambermaid they'd barely noticed earlier.

She felt a little queasy as the helicopter made its swaying ascent into the sky but soon they were up amid the stars, looking down onto the twinkling lights of L'Idylle, and Hannah looked around her, breathless with wonder.

'Ever been in one of these before?' questioned Kulal above the sound of the clattering blades.

Hannah was so engrossed in the view that she spoke without thinking. 'What do you think?'

Despite her undeniable lack of protocol, Kulal smiled. How refreshing it was to be out with someone so deliciously unsophisticated! Instead of hanging onto his every word, she was sitting exclaiming about the beauty of the stars. Unless that was an attempt to convince him that she had *depth*. He felt a slight whisper of self-admonishment as he acknowledged his own cynicism, wondering when such a jaded attitude had fixed itself firmly in his heart and taken root there.

You know when, he thought, unable to prevent the rush of memory which still had the power to make his heart clench with pain. *When your mother took the ultimate revenge on your father and destroyed your faith in women for ever.*

Did she feel his eyes on her? Was that why she turned, a look of uncertainty crossing over her face, as if she'd just remembered where she was—and who she was with. 'You haven't told me anything about this party,' she said.

'Like what?'

'Well, like who's throwing it, for a start.'

He leaned forward to alleviate the need to shout above the clatter of the blades. 'An Italian property tycoon called Salvatore di Luca, who happens to be one of my oldest friends,' he said huskily, his throat growing dry as the subtle fragrance of her perfume had a predictable if unwanted effect on his senses. 'I first met him when I was studying in Norway.'

'What were you studying?'

It was a long time since anyone had asked him that, but the interest in her eyes looked genuine. 'A Master's degree in energy and natural resources.'

'Gosh. That sounds very high-powered. Did you like it?'

Kulal tensed. As much as it would have been possible to have liked anything at that time. He had used the course as an escape from the unbearable events at home, but he wouldn't tell her that. He never talked about that. Not even with his twin brother, who had found her. Who had…

He cleared his throat, but it didn't quite remove the bitter taste in his mouth. 'I liked it well enough and it has been very useful to me in my role as Sheikh. Salvatore and I were on the same course and we've stayed in touch, although our lives are very different. He lives in Rome but has a holiday place here in Sardinia.'

'So what's the party in aid of?'

'Why, me, of course,' he said softly. 'Once my old friend discovered I was working on the island, he wanted to show me some of the hospitality for which he is renowned.'

'You don't sound overjoyed about the prospect.'

He shrugged, as he spoke in a rare moment of candour. 'Sometimes it becomes rather tedious always to be the focal point of people's attention at these events.'

She chewed her lip. 'So how are you planning to explain me?'

A slow smile curved his lips. 'Oh, don't you worry about that. I never have to explain anything,' he said arrogantly. 'Nobody need know your true identity. Tonight you can be whoever you want to be, Hannah.'

Hannah's heart pounded. It felt as if he were waving another magic wand—a continuation of the spell which had made her into this glossy woman travelling by helicopter to a party. It was exciting but it was scary, too. She stole a glimpse at his hawk-like profile, knowing that she mustn't make the mistake of believing this was real. Or that the desert King in the dark dress suit really *was* her date for the night.

The helicopter dipped downwards towards a pad fringed with burning torches where an imposing man was waiting to greet them—the flames painting his face with bronze and gold. The wind plastered Hannah's dress against her legs as they emerged from the helicopter and her carefully dried hair blew wildly around her shoulders. Salvatore di Luca greeted Kulal with affection but his words to her were cursory—as if it was a waste of his time getting to know her. As if she was just one in a long line of women Kulal had brought to parties over the years.

Well, of course she was!

Taking care not to trip in her spindly sandals,

Hannah followed the two men onto a terrace where the milling guests were assembled near the swimming pool. Tall trees were lit with fairy lights and flower-strewn tables were decked with candles whose flames barely flickered in the stillness of the evening air. The momentary silence which greeted their appearance was followed by a burst of excited chatter and Hannah could feel countless eyes boring into her. And suddenly she understood exactly what Kulal had meant. It *was* disconcerting to be the focus of everyone's attention and she wondered if people could tell she was wearing a borrowed dress and jewels.

The sultry sound of jazz began to drift through the air and a voluptuous singer in a silver dress began warming up. Over by the gin bar Hannah could see a Hollywood A-lister who'd recently been dating a woman half his age—and surely that was a famously tearaway European princess doing an impressive yoga pose by the side of the swimming pool?

And that was when the fun really began. Well, for everyone except her. She seemed to be the only person who didn't know anybody else and it was all too easy for Hannah to become tongue-tied. Her nerves weren't helped by the fact that she happened to be with the most important person at the party and he was the only person they wanted to talk to. Even when Kulal introduced her to people, their interest was polite rather than genuine. A couple of times, she got shoved aside as if she was an impediment to the main attraction, but she acted as if it hadn't happened, her smile as determinedly bright as the one she used at work if she happened to walk in on a couple having sex, who hadn't bothered to put the 'Do Not Disturb' sign on the door.

But when a sparky blonde came up and started chattering to Kulal in what was obviously his native tongue, Hannah gave up. Why fight it? Why bother reaching for something which could never be hers? Didn't matter how well she scrubbed up in the borrowed finery—it was all superficial. She was still the chambermaid. Still the outsider. Always had been and probably always would be.

Unnoticed, she walked across the crowded

terrace and perched on the edge of a fountain so that she could people-watch and listen to the band. She saw people hovering around Kulal and couldn't deny the sudden wistful punch to her heart as she surveyed his powerful physique and jet-dark hair. But the music and the scent of jasmine were pleasures in themselves and Hannah sat sipping at her cocktail, in which floated tiny violet flowers. She watched a waitress tottering along the edge of the swimming pool carrying a tray of drinks, a deliberate sway of her curvy bottom as she passed the Sheikh only adding to her precarious posture.

She's going to drop those if she isn't careful, thought Hannah anxiously, just as the loud crash of crystal hitting marble tiles shattered the buzz of the party.

It was almost comic, the way everyone stared at the waitress scrabbling around amid the debris, as if she were an alien who'd just fallen from space. Quickly, Hannah put her glass down and went to help, crouching down and stilling the woman's shaking fingers, terrified she was going to slice her hand open. The chatter resumed as Hannah took over the clear-up operation, becoming so engrossed in her task that it wasn't until she'd dropped the final piece of crystal onto the tray that she suddenly became aware of someone standing over her.

Looking up, she met Kulal's bemused expression and was still so caught up in what she was doing that she spoke to him almost absently. 'Do you think you could get me a dustpan and brush from somewhere?'

'A dustpan and what?' he echoed incredulously.

She realised he didn't have a clue what she was talking about and was wondering how to explain what it was—perhaps by some elaborate form of charade—when a waiter came over and started berating the waitress in a torrent of furious French.

'Come,' said Kulal firmly, pulling her to her feet. 'I think you've done quite enough. Let them sort it out among themselves. Unless you're planning to put on an apron and take over her job for the rest of the evening? Do you ever stop working, Hannah?'

In the darkness, Hannah blushed as she registered his sardonic tone. 'I couldn't just leave the poor girl to struggle by herself—and nobody else was bothering to help, were they?'

'Not everybody here has your skill-set,' he said drily.

She realised that his hand was at her elbow and he was leading her away from the curious eyes of the onlookers, towards the shadowed lawns which stretched out behind the swimming pool. It was peaceful here. And deserted, too. She could still hear the music, but it was just her and Kulal—who had a look on his face which was mid-way between irritation and amusement.

'Are you enjoying the party?' he questioned.

'It was very kind of you to bring me.'

'That wasn't what I asked, Hannah.'

Awkwardly, she shrugged. 'I'm glad I came.'

'Oh?'

She hesitated, but something in the piercing gleam of his black eyes made her answer his question truthfully. 'It made me realise that high-society parties aren't all they're cracked up to be.'

'And why might that be?'

She hesitated only for a second. 'Well, nobody really talks about anything very much, do they? All the men seemed so competitive and most of the women were all over you like a rash, which made me think that bringing me here wasn't as effective as you'd hoped. Or maybe I'm cramping your style.' She looked at him questioningly. 'In which case, I could easily make myself scarce until you're ready to go, if that's what you want.'

Kulal felt a tug of admiration. He'd heard people around him exclaiming in horror when the little chambermaid had been crouching down, careless of the way her costly dress had been rucked up around her bare thighs, yet he had admired the way she had leapt to the defence of the hapless waitress. And now, instead of plying him with saccharine words of gratitude, she was echoing his very own sentiments about these kinds of occasions.

His eyes narrowed. People rarely told him what

he needed to hear—only what they thought he *wanted* to hear, and the two were rarely the same. And suddenly the desire to feel her in his arms was overwhelming. Too overwhelming to resist—and why should he? What harm would it do? 'Dance with me instead,' he said.

Hannah blinked at him. 'What, here?'

'Right here.'

Perhaps if he'd insisted on taking her to the small dance floor in front of the band, where they would have been visible to the other partygoers, Hannah might have refused. But he didn't. He just pulled her into his arms as if he danced on moonlit lawns every night of the week and every bit of apprehension drained from her body. Because what woman would have objected to being held by the Sheikh like this? Hadn't this been one of the forbidden fantasies she'd tried not to have while she'd been working for him? Only she was discovering that sometimes reality exceeded the fantasy—exceeded it in a way which was outside her understanding.

Suddenly, the dance seemed irrelevant to what

was happening inside her body. Her nipples had become rock-hard and she wondered if he could feel them pushing insistently against his dress shirt. And now there was a distracting ache, low in her belly, and she knew she needed to stop this before she did something she regretted—like whispering her lips along the darkened edge of his jaw and begging him to kiss her. Her cheeks were burning as she pulled away from him and she met the hectic glitter of his dark gaze.

'I think I'd better go back now,' she said huskily. 'To the hotel, I mean.'

'Oh?' On the shadowed lawn, he raised a laconic eyebrow. 'Why?'

You know why. Because you're making me want things I have no right to want. Because I'm a virgin and you're a man of the world and I've spent my whole life being cautious.

'I'm tired,' she said.

He must have known it was an excuse, but he didn't query it. Maybe he realised that it was the right thing to do. Or the only thing to do. There was a brief silence before he nodded. 'Okay. I could use an early night myself. Let's go.'

And wasn't human nature unpredictable? Because as soon as Kulal agreed to her request, Hannah began to regret her decision. Couldn't she have danced with him a bit longer? Enjoyed what was happening without making such a big deal of it and bringing the evening to such an abrupt end?

The waiting helicopter whisked them back through the starry skies and her heart was racing as they crept through the hotel corridors. But they managed to slip into Kulal's private elevator and make it back to the penthouse suite without being seen. The usual inscrutable bodyguards lined the corridor but Hannah had become so used to seeing them that she barely gave them a second glance. She came to a halt outside the door to her room and stared up into Kulal's carved features, wondering if she ought to offer to turn down his bed for him before she retired for the night. Until she drew herself up short. Was she *crazy*? Was she planning to tiptoe into his vast bedroom and leave a chocolate on the pillowcase?

'Thank you very much for the evening, Your Royal Highness,' she said formally as she pushed the door open. 'I'll put the dress, shoes and necklace into a bag and drop it off first thing and now I'll say goodnight.'

The Sheikh didn't appear to be listening; he was too busy looking over her shoulder into her room, his black eyes thoughtful. 'It's very small,' he observed, his gaze skating over the narrow bed and functional furniture.

'Of course it's small,' she said defensively. 'I'm staff, remember?'

But Kulal wasn't really thinking about her status right then. He wasn't really thinking about anything other than the frustration which was heating his blood and refusing to be cooled by reason. He had been very turned on during that tantalisingly brief dance and, despite all his best intentions, had been contemplating brushing his fingertips over her luscious breasts when she'd pulled away and told him she wanted to go home.

He remembered feeling startled because that had never happened before—not unless it was with the expectation that they would quickly adjourn to the nearest bedroom. But not with this little chambermaid. She was primly saying goodnight to him as though that was exactly what she wanted, even though the darkening of her aquamarine eyes left him in no doubt that their desire was mutual.

If he was being sensible, he would turn away. Go to his room and kill off his ardour with an icy shower. And maybe, instead of flying straight to Zahristan tomorrow, he could take a detour via Sweden—call in on that delicious blonde actress he'd never got around to bedding a few years back. Hadn't she sent him a text the other day, disingenuously saying she was sorry to hear about his recent relationship break-up? He thought what else she had written as a postscript, making it graphically clear she wanted him as her lover.

But he didn't want that woman with her bony hips which would grind into a man's flesh like weapons. He wanted softness and voluptuousness. Lush breasts he could bury his head in and a trembling mouth he could plunder to his heart's content. For the first time in his life, he wanted someone who was outside his realm of experience—was it novelty value which made him hunger for the little chambermaid so much?

He pulled Hannah into his arms and saw her eyes widen as he began to run his fingertip down her spine.

'Kulal?' she whispered.

'Yes?' he whispered back, lowering his head so that their mouths were centimetres apart. He was close enough to kiss her, but he paused long enough to allow her to shake her head. To give her a second opportunity to pull away from him. Because that was the right thing to do, even if every atom in his hungry body rebelled against such an idea.

But she didn't pull away. Her lips parted and as lust fired in his belly, he knew he wasn't going to take her back to his own bedroom. That he had no desire to walk past the line of bodyguards stationed there, even though they had witnessed countless transgressions such as this in the past. And maybe it was better this way. Less intimidating for her—and certainly more novel for him. He pulled her a little closer and felt his erection grow even harder.

'Wh-what are you doing, Kulal?' she questioned breathlessly.

It occurred to him that women were rarely original at moments like this. What did she think he was doing—writing a research paper on solar energy? He allowed his lips to drift over the silky texture of her neck, his words muffled by the lazy indulgence of that first, slow kiss. 'I think we both know the answer to that question. I'm going to make love to you, that's if you want me to—which I think you do.'

Hannah swallowed, trying to fight the feelings which were fluttering inside her. She should tell him to stop before this went any further. Before he started to touch her trembling breasts, which were aching to be touched. But she couldn't. She just couldn't. How could she turn her back on something which felt so wonderful? The most wonderful thing she'd ever experienced. She hadn't realised that being in a man's arms could make you feel like this—as if you could leap up into the air and just *fly*. She made a helpless little sound as his mouth brushed along her jaw and her eyelids flickered to a close. Was that his *tongue* she could feel, trailing an erotic and moist little path over her skin? She shivered as he did it again. Yes, it was.

She wasn't sure if he was waiting for some kind of response, but she guessed she gave one when she suddenly folded her arms tightly around his shoulders.

'I'm taking it that's a yes?' he said on a low growl.

'It's certainly not a no,' she said, with a boldness she hadn't known she possessed.

He laughed as he stepped inside and kicked the door shut behind them and then he was kissing her properly. Or maybe that should have been improperly. His hands were sliding over her silky dress as he murmured something in a language she didn't understand. But maybe she didn't need to. Maybe this was something which was meant to be enjoyed without commitment or expectation. And didn't they say that the language of love was universal?

She should have felt shy as he slid her zip down and peeled the delicate dress from her body, but she didn't. Not when it seemed that her voluptuous curves pleased him. The stylist who had transformed her had insisted on matching underwear and Hannah was glad now that she had agreed. Glad she was wearing a deceptively delicate bra which disguised the fact that it had needed to do a lot of elemental support work. Deftly, he unclipped it and as her breasts came spilling out, he gave another appreciative murmur before locking his hot lips around one thrusting nipple. Hannah gasped—she couldn't help it. She felt as if she'd taken a one-way trip to heaven. As if she'd found something she hadn't believed existed. And suddenly she wanted to touch *him*. To feel the Sheikh's skin beneath her fingers.

With the nimbleness which had made her the finest chambermaid in the Granchester group, she slid free the mother-of-pearl buttons to liberate his powerful chest, her hands running greedily over the hard muscle which sheathed the silken skin. Was that what made him groan like that? What made him pick her up as if she were composed of nothing heavier than feathers, before carrying her towards the tiny single bed and depositing her on the mattress?

And still she didn't feel shy—not even as he removed the clothes from his body, his eyes not leaving her face. Nor when he was completely naked and leaning over to slither her panties all the way down her thighs and she felt cool air wash over her naked skin. There was no time to feel anything—other than a joyful recognition of the greedy hunger which was spiralling up inside her, so that when Kulal lay down on top of her—because the bed wasn't really big enough for any other kind of combination—all Hannah could do was to give a shuddering little moan of relief.

'You like that?' he said, a smile playing around the edges of his lips as he gazed down at her, his hand between her thighs.

Was he referring to the fact that she could feel his blunt hardness pushing unashamedly against her belly? Or was it one of those questions which didn't really require an answer—not when he was now discovering the molten heat between her legs with a finger which was making her writhe with pleasure?

'This is crazy!' Hannah gasped. 'I can't—'

'Oh, yes, you can,' he said, his tongue snaking over her breasts until her nipples felt as if they were going to explode.

And who was she to contradict him, when their bodies seemed to fit together as if they had been made for each other? When she was so hungry for him that she even managed to giggle as he clumsily tore open what was obviously protection and heard him give a muffled curse. She didn't stop to think, or to question why he just *happened* to be carrying a condom around with him because for the first time in her life, Hannah hadn't just stepped outside her comfort zone—she'd taken a great flying leap into unknown territory.

And she loved it.

She loved everything about it. Kissing him and touching him. Running her fingers through the tousled splendour of his thick black hair. Skating her palms over the honed planes of his spectacular body until he bit out that he couldn't take much more. Suddenly, she wasn't humble Hannah Wilson any more—but a woman who seemed to be able to drive this hawk-faced man wild with desire. Her initial shyness had been melted away by their rapidly growing intimacy, and suddenly Hannah realised he was pushing her thighs open to enter her.

The next few seconds were a bit of a blur. There was a little bit of pain—though not very much. And there was undeniable surprise on the face of the Sheikh as he stilled, mid-thrust. But then their bodies seemed to take over and everything else got forgotten when he started moving again until she was gasping out words she hadn't realised she knew. She heard herself making broken little pleas as she hovered on the edge of something which seemed tantalisingly out of reach.

But at last she found it. And it wasn't just what

she had thought it might be—it was more. So much more. She gave a disbelieving cry, and as she began to convulse around the Sheikh's thrusting hardness, he gave a low and exultant shout of his own. And as Hannah felt his big body quivering with pleasure, she found herself thinking that she never wanted this night to end.

CHAPTER FOUR

'SO WHEN WERE you planning to tell me?'

Swallowing down the nausea which was rising in her throat, Hannah looked at her little sister, trying not to react to the accusing stare which had accompanied her accusing words. Trying to convince herself that Tamsyn couldn't possibly *know*—not when she'd only just found out herself.

'Tell you what?' she questioned weakly.

'About your pregnancy, of course,' hissed Tamsyn. 'Or were you planning to keep it a great big secret until you were just about to pop?'

Hannah swallowed again, only this time the saltiness in her throat felt suspiciously like the taste of tears—and she'd convinced herself she wasn't going to cry. She wasn't, she thought fiercely. Because tears wouldn't solve anything. She'd learnt that the hard way.

'How did you know?' she whispered.

'Hello? Are you *serious*?' Tamsyn filled up the kettle, not appearing to notice that she was splashing water all over Hannah's carefully polished tiles. 'It must be obvious to everyone.'

'Nobody at the Granchester knows,' said Hannah quickly.

'Really? Well, maybe the other staff don't have eyes in their heads or maybe I just know you better than anyone, but it's as obvious to me as the nose on your face. Look at you, Hannah—your breasts are enormous and your complexion looks green…'

'Thanks,' said Hannah tonelessly.

'I can't believe it. You, of all people.'

'What's that supposed to mean?'

Tamsyn shrugged. 'You're the one who was always so good. Who never put a foot wrong.'

Hannah didn't answer, just stared up into her sister's bewildered face. It was true. She'd been the model child. The peacemaker. The quiet one who had learnt that saying as little as possible and pretending the bad stuff wasn't happening was the best way for things to get back to normal. Whatever normal was. But this was one situation where pretending it wasn't happening wasn't going to work.

'So who's the daddy, Hannah?' continued Tamsyn. 'I didn't even realise you were in a relationship.'

Because she wasn't in a relationship, that was why. Hannah leaned back in the armchair and closed her eyes, not wanting to betray her fear, knowing that sooner or later she was going to have to come clean. To say the words out loud. Because words would make it real. They would confirm what up until now had just been a nagging fear.

She was pregnant.

She was carrying the desert King's child beneath her thundering heart.

Her mind took her back to that crazy night when Kulal had laid her down on that narrow single bed, his black eyes full of intent as he had run a careless thumb over her thrusting nipple. What had happened next had seemed inevitable—but that wasn't really true. She could have stopped him. He'd given her every opportunity to do so, but she had just carried on regardless. She had broken every rule in the book—and she wasn't just thinking about the Granchester's strict policy of not fraternising with guests. Hadn't she clung onto her virginity as if it was something very precious? Hadn't it been a big deal for her, having seen what the fallout from casual sex could be? While most women her age seemed content to be free with their bodies, Hannah had been the opposite—as prim as a woman from a different age.

And she had surrendered all that innocence to a man who had simply taken it as his due! Who afterwards had looked at the ceiling with a reflective look on his hawk-like features.

'I've never done it in such a narrow bed before,' he had observed thoughtfully, his fingers sliding between her thighs and easing them apart. 'I think it adds a certain *something*.'

But even that arrogant boast hadn't been enough

to kill her hunger for him. Instead, she had just turned to him with silent invitation in her eyes and he'd done it to her all over again. And again. She remembered the intensity of feelings which had seemed to explode inside her, like a bomb which been waiting a long time to be detonated. Was that why she had responded like someone she didn't really know—showing a side of herself she hadn't realised existed? Like a wildcat, she thought guiltily. Like…

She remembered what he'd said, just before the first time.

'You want this, Hannah?'

'Yes.'

'And so do I. But it's one night only—do you understand? Not just because I am a king and you a chambermaid, and our positions in life are so incompatible. The truth is that I've just come out of a relationship and I'm not looking for another one. If you want more than that, I cannot give it to you and I'll walk out of this room right now and leave you alone, no matter how hard I might find it.'

But Hannah had been powerless to resist him. How could she have resisted him when just looking into those gleaming black eyes had made her want to melt?

'One night is fine with me,' she had whispered back.

'So who's the daddy?' repeated Tamsyn, cutting impatiently into Hannah's uncomfortable thoughts.

And that was when Hannah realised that the tables were turned for the first time in their lives. That Tamsyn, for all her wildness, had never presented with a problem as big as this. A problem which seemed insurmountable. Which had made her thoughts spin with increasing desperation, ever since she'd first seen that blue line on the pregnancy test.

'You won't be able to keep it a secret for ever, you know.' Tamsyn poured boiling water into the teapot before looking up. 'Is it that bloke who works in the accounts department—the one you got off with at the Christmas party?'

Hannah shuddered. No way. That particular

encounter had ended humiliatingly when he'd shoved his hand up her jumper and she'd jumped away and told him she didn't want sex in the stationery cupboard, and he had sneered and told her she was fat and frigid.

She certainly hadn't jumped away in horror when Kulal had touched her, had she?

But she knew Tamsyn was right. She couldn't keep it a secret. She had no right to do that. And wasn't the truth of it that if she disregarded her thoughtless and stupid behaviour… She swallowed again. If she thought about the *reality* rather than the repercussions—then she couldn't deny the unexpected sense of excitement which was bubbling away inside her. She was going to have a baby and she would love and protect that baby with all her heart, just as she'd done for her little sister—no matter what obstacles lay ahead.

'His name is Kulal.' For the first time since she'd lain in his arms she said his name out loud and even as she uttered it, she thought how bizarre it was that her very first lover should have been the influential desert King.

'Nice name,' said Tamsyn approvingly. 'What's he like?'

And here it was—in all its unvarnished and frankly unbelievable truth.

'He's…well, he's very powerful and dynamic.'

'Really?'

She heard the doubt in Tamsyn's voice which she couldn't quite disguise and, for the first time in her life, Hannah wasn't sure how to respond. Because she had always been the one who came armed with words of wisdom. Words to soothe and comfort. There hadn't been a single bad situation during their growing up which she hadn't felt equipped to deal with.

Until now.

Had she been guilty of thinking she was so clever—so *invulnerable*—that she would never find herself in a situation like this? Well, here was reality—about to teach her the hardest lesson of all.

'He's a sheikh,' she said.

Tamsyn screwed up her face. 'What are you talking about?'

Hannah swallowed. 'The father of my baby. He's a…' She cleared her throat because not only did it sound unbelievable—it also sounded slightly grandiose. 'A desert king,' she finished quietly.

She could see that Tamsyn was trying not to laugh, but then the gravity of the situation must have hit her and the smile was wiped from her sister's wide mouth. 'This is no joking matter,' she said crossly.

'I'm not joking—he *is* a desert king.'

'Hannah.' Tamsyn glared. 'You're not experienced. You don't realise what men are like. They say all kinds of things when they're trying to get a woman to—'

'He *is*!' declared Hannah, with an uncharacteristic burst of fervour because usually, she trod carefully where Tamsyn was concerned. 'He's called Sheikh Kulal Al Diya and he's the King of Zahristan.'

'Good…*grief*.' There was a pause and then, the tea-making forgotten, Tamsyn slumped against the sink, her eyes wide. 'Not…not the one in the papers who was described as—'

'One of the world's most eligible bachelors?' supplied Hannah. 'Yes, that's him.'

'But…how? I mean, *how*?'

The question was well-meant, but it hurt. Because Tamsyn's incredulity said a lot. It said: how could someone like Kulal have possibly become involved with a woman like *her*? Yet Hannah was in no position to criticise her sister's disbelief, when she felt pretty much that way herself.

'He needed a partner to take to a fancy party.'

'And he chose *you*?'

Hannah drew her shoulders back and spoke to Tamsyn with uncharacteristic coolness. 'Yes, he did. I was working for him.'

'As a chambermaid?'

'As a chambermaid,' Hannah agreed tightly. 'I was assigned to work solely for him. Sometimes we used to chat about stuff. We got on quite… well.'

Tamsyn gave a raucous laugh. 'I'll say. So you went off to a party with him and…?'

'I'm not going to spell it out for you, Tamsyn—it's pretty obvious what happened.'

Tamsyn looked momentarily surprised—as if this new and rather bolshie sister, who usually trod so carefully, was taking a little getting used to. She nodded. 'So what are you planning to do?'

Hannah hesitated before answering because this was the bit she still wasn't quite clear about. Because the moment she told him, she would lose control over the situation. Instinct told her that. Kulal wasn't just a powerful man—he was also a desert king and weren't royals notoriously possessive about their heirs? The truth was that she didn't know how he would respond because she didn't really know *him*. He might try to take control of her and the baby. He might deny all responsibility and send her packing. In many ways, it would be easier all round if she just crept away and brought up the baby on her own without bothering to tell him.

A long sigh escaped from her lips. It would be easier, yes—but deep down she knew she couldn't go through with it. Because Hannah had grown up never knowing or meeting her father, and she knew all about the huge emotional hole that could leave at the centre of a child's existence. There were risks involved in letting him know—of course there were—but these were risks she had to take.

'I'm going to tell him, of course,' she said. 'As soon as you've gone, I'm going to telephone him.'

The only problem being that she didn't actually have a number for him, because he hadn't given her one. Well, why would he, when he'd never been intending to see her again? There had been one final, lingering kiss and Hannah, completely exhausted after their energetic night, had fallen into a deep sleep. And when she'd woken up, he was gone. The penthouse suite along the corridor had been cleared of all evidence that Kulal had stayed there. The bodyguards had disappeared and so had the Sheikh's luggage. Even the fancy dress and priceless necklace were gone, presumably on their way back to the stylist. It might have all been a dream, were it not for the pleasurable aching of her body. And yet she had still been suffering from some kind of delusion, hadn't she? There had still been a stupid part of her which had wondered if he might have left her a note or *something.*

But whisking her way around his suite—supposedly giving it the most thorough cleaning of its life—had failed to produce any kind of sentiment that Kulal Al Diya would ever give her another thought. Hannah had felt flat—there was no denying it. It had been the most spectacular introduction to sex and now she was going to have to resign herself to her usual frigid life. Yet it had been more than that. In his arms, she had felt like a woman who was capable of anything. He had been tender with her. And passionate. In fact, he had been everything a woman dreamt a man could be.

Maybe it was easy to be that way when you knew you were never going to see someone again. When you knew that you weren't even going to have to speak to them in the morning. She told herself she should be grateful he'd just crept away in the early hours, because the reality of waking up in that cramped staff bedroom would have been embarrassing. Would she have boiled the electric kettle which was jammed onto one of the shelves and offered to make him a mug of herb tea? Then watched as he put on his clothes and tried to make his escape as quickly as possible?

She'd tried to feel indignant that he'd beat such a hasty retreat, but she couldn't quite bring herself to be angry with him. Had she somehow been aware—on a deep, subliminal level—that the cells of his child were already multiplying rapidly inside her? Was that why she found it so difficult to stop thinking about him, with a heart that beat a little too fast and a soft yearning which made her feel uncomfortable?

But Hannah knew that feelings passed. All of them. And that eventually the intensity of what was happening to you faded with time. She'd told herself to be grateful that nobody at the Granchester had found out and her job was safe. She'd got away with it, scot-free. Or so she'd thought. She had worked for two more weeks at the Sardinian hotel before returning to London, just in time to discover that her period was late and to try to deny to herself why that might be. Until denial was no longer an option…

Hannah clicked onto the Zahristan website but, naturally, there was no handy link to the King's email account. She found the number of the Embassy in London and tried ringing, in the hope of being able to convey a subtle message through one of the diplomats. But the phone system was automated and her dilemma didn't fall into the category of someone visiting the country who was chasing up their visa. She supposed she could mail Kulal a letter and emblazon it with 'private and confidential'—but there was no guaranteeing he would receive it unopened. The embassy might think it was from a crackpot and even if they didn't, it meant that the Sheikh would discover he was going to be a father *after* his staff had found out. Hannah knew very little about royal protocol, but even she could recognise that would be a big mistake. A very big mistake.

She needed to tell him in person—but how?

There *was* a solution—to use the money she'd been squirrelling away since she'd first started work. The little sums of money which had grown, bit by bit, into a halfway decent sum which would one day become a deposit on a home of her own.

Could she break into it to buy herself an airline ticket to Zahristan?

Her heart began to pound. There was no other option—because how else was she going to get to see Kulal? But that money was sacrosanct and symbolic. She'd promised herself she would never touch it and now fear washed over her as she realised that once again she wasn't playing safe. Because this wasn't risk-averse Hannah. This was more of the same Hannah who had leapt into bed with the desert King, when deep down she'd known she shouldn't. Her hand went down to cradle her belly because she knew she had little choice. She'd protected Tamsyn when they had been growing up—just as she would protect her baby now. She didn't know how Kulal would respond, but that wasn't her problem. She needed to give their child the best possible chance—and everything else was outside her control.

And surely he would have the decency to refund her air fare?

Which was how she ended up in a plane, crossing the Murjaan Sea and heading towards the Sheikh's homeland.

She was fortunate that Zahristan had opened its borders a decade ago, after winning the war with neighbouring Quzabar, and fortunate that she had enough annual leave to book herself a last-minute break. She couldn't decide if it was good fortune or fate that her visa-acquiring trip to the Zahristan Embassy had introduced her to a helpful woman called Elissa. Elissa had informed her that visitors were allowed access to the Sheikh's palace every Tuesday and Thursday afternoon, and His Royal Highness was actively encouraging trips from foreign visitors. At this, Hannah's heart had leapt—because surely she could engineer some kind of meeting if she gained access to Kulal's home.

After consulting a weather map, she discovered that the temperature of her destination was roasting and so she used some more of her precious savings to buy some suitable clothes. Inexpensive clothes in natural fabrics in light colours which wouldn't absorb the heat. Clothes which would disguise her tender breasts which were the only outward sign of her pregnancy. But most important of all—new clothes which meant she wouldn't turn up at a fancy palace looking like a tramp.

The flight was long and her limbs felt cramped, because she hadn't wanted to squander any of her precious money upgrading her seat. She tried distracting herself by reading what was supposed to be the definitive history of Zahristan, but the clunky paragraphs didn't manage to hold her attention for long. For a long time, the book lay open on the same page as she wondered what would happen when she finally gained access to Kulal. Would she be thrown in some dark jail—forced to wait for the British consulate to come and bail her out and put her on the next flight to

England, with a fierce lecture on compromising international diplomacy ringing in her ears?

But even if the worst happened and she didn't get within a hundred yards of him, at least she would have tried.

Hannah stared out of the plane window—at the seemingly endless expanse of desert. As the aircraft began to descend, she could see the welcome green of palm trees and in the distance a gleam of water, surrounded by tents. And now they were approaching a city—with turrets and gleaming spires, just like in a fairy tale. There were flashes of blue and lots of gold. This must be Ashkhazar, which she'd just read about. A rich city with a troubled history. Hadn't Kulal mentioned it briefly when she had run her fingertip over the raised scar which ran from nipple to groin and was the only blemish which marred his perfect body? But he hadn't wanted to talk about what had caused it. The truth was he hadn't wanted to talk about anything much, except how much he liked her breasts. Well, he was going to have to talk about his baby, whether he liked it or not.

And then her stomach gave a flip as the airport watchtower grew closer and she closed her eyes as the huge aircraft began to swoop towards the runway.

CHAPTER FIVE

FROM BEHIND THE tinted windows of his heavily bullet-proofed car, Kulal watched the plane land and he felt a wave of anger as the passengers began to disembark.

He saw her immediately—instantly recognisable, and not just because she was the only woman travelling solo.

Did she really think she could sneak into his homeland without him getting wind of it?

Her head was uncovered, but at least her shoulders were not bare. She was wearing a pale dress which hung almost to her ankles. It was a modest dress, even by Zahristan standards, but it failed to disguise the generous curve of her breasts or the womanly swell of her buttocks, and Kulal's jaw tightened. It would be easier all round if he simply had her brought to his car for the short drive to the city but that might amount to something resembling an official welcome and he would not countenance that. He watched as another black limousine edged onto the tarmac and one of his most trusted aides got out of the car.

Kulal spoke rapidly to his driver. 'Wait until Najib gets her into the limousine,' he bit out. 'And then tail them.'

'Yes, sire.'

He didn't say another word during the journey which followed, his eyes fixed resolutely on the car in front of them as they drove at speed through the wide roads which led into the city. When the first limousine drew to a halt, he could see the look of consternation on Hannah's face as she gazed up at the impressive gilded façade of the famous building and for a moment, he wondered if she might refuse to go inside and then what would they do? But Najib was a master at getting people to carry out his master's wishes and within minutes, she was walking up the marble steps, while yet another aide carried her single suitcase.

He waited for several minutes before discreetly entering the building, two of his bodyguards tailing him like shadows. But as the elevator ascended, Kulal found his thoughts drifting back to another similar ride—when he had been obsessed by the rise and fall of Hannah's magnificent breasts, covered in the delicate silk of the dress he had ordered for her to wear to the party. Had he been completely insane? Carried away by what he'd convinced himself was nothing but an altruistic action to give the little chambermaid a well-deserved treat, without bothering to examine the real motive of desire which was bubbling beneath the surface of his intentions? Probably. His mouth hardened into a grim mockery of a smile. Didn't they say that men were architects of their own destruction?

The elevator doors opened and as he strode along the corridor he saw Najib standing sentry outside a door, his face inscrutable.

'What did she say?' questioned Kulal as he grew close, and Najib gave a brief bow before shrugging.

'She was a little *militant* at first, sire—but then she seemed to grow resigned to her fate and offered no resistance.'

'Good. Let us hope that state of affairs continues. Stand back, Najib.'

'Should I not accompany you inside, sire?'

Briefly, Kulal's lips curved. 'You think the little Englishwoman will attack me?'

'I thought I saw fire in her eyes, sire.'

Kulal's lips hardened. 'The fire will soon be doused, Najib. Make no mistake about that.'

He pushed open the door and saw Hannah. She was standing by the window, as if she had been staring out onto the magnificent mixture of ancient and new to be found in the city streets outside. At the sound of the door closing, she whirled round and his first thought was that Najib had been right. That was definitely fire he could see in her eyes—something he had not witnessed in all the time she had serviced his penthouse suite. The blaze of aquamarine as she glared at him almost dazzled him and she must have been shaking her head because gleaming strands of mahogany hair had broken free from the confinement of their elastic band and were tumbling in glorious disarray around her shoulders. For a few distracting seconds, he felt the instant flare of lust before instinctively subduing it. Because wasn't it lust which had got him into this predicament?

'Would you mind telling me what is going on?' she demanded, her voice rising. 'Why I was bundled off the plane and into a waiting car as if I was some sort of criminal? And why I've been brought here—to this fancy hotel—when I have a room reservation at the Souk Vista Hostel?'

Kulal had been anticipating many reactions, but such a feisty question from a woman of her stature only confirmed his suspicions about the reason for her journey. His eyes narrowed, for although he had encountered determination from ex-lovers many times in the past—nobody had ever been quite as audacious as Hannah Wilson. Well, she would soon discover that coming here had been a big mistake. A very big mistake.

'I assume you wanted to see me,' he said coolly.

'So I thought I would curtail any unnecessary time-wasting by bringing you straight here.'

'When your aide said…' For a moment her confidence appeared to waver. 'When he said he was taking me to the palace…'

Kulal's lips curved into a smile he fully intended to be cruel because now he was dealing with something he'd encountered ever since he first became aware that his blood was blue, and he was in possession of connections most people could only dream of. Was that what Hannah ultimately wanted? he wondered cynically. A share of his unimaginable riches and access to his privileged life? In which case, perhaps it was necessary to teach her a small lesson—just to set the matter straight before she let her imagination run away with itself. 'And you thought they meant they were bringing you to my palace?' he queried, his gaze deliberately lingering on the golden logo of a crown which was embroidered onto one of the napkins which adorned a gleaming table. 'Rather than the Royal Palace Hotel?'

The dull flush of her cheeks told Kulal his guess

had been accurate and, mockingly, he raised his eyebrows. 'I hope you aren't too disappointed, Hannah. Did you think our one night together would entitle you to enjoy some of the perks of having a royal lover? And that I would be taking you on a sightseeing tour of the fabled gardens of my palace, or dipping into the Al Diya jewellery collection to present you with a precious bauble?'

'Of course not,' she said stiffly.

'I thought you would feel more at home in a hotel,' he added carelessly. 'And of course, it carries the extra benefit of not compromising me in any way.'

It was the most patronising thing she'd ever heard and Hannah had to suck in a deep breath to stop herself from shaking, telling herself that nothing would be achieved by giving into the rage which was smouldering inside her, like a fire which refused to die. Because showing your feelings made you vulnerable—and she had the scars to prove it. Letting emotion get the better of you was a bad idea. Remaining cool and calm was the first law of survival—she knew that.

But although she'd spent most of her life following that creed, she wasn't finding it so easy right now. Were her fluctuating hormones once again to blame—making her react in a way which was alien to her? Or did none of the usual rules apply now that she had an unborn child to protect?

Because things were different now and she needed to recognise that. When she'd been looking after Tamsyn, she'd been nothing but a child herself and her options had been limited. But she was an adult now. She might not have Kulal's material wealth or power, but she was resourceful as only someone in a dilemma could be and would not be treated like some docile little prisoner.

So stick to the facts.

'You don't even know why I'm here,' she said.

'Of course I do.'

She blinked at him and gulped. 'You do?'

'Oh, Hannah.' He gave a short laugh before his hawk-like features hardened into a cynical expression. 'You wouldn't need to be a genius to work it out. You've decided that you're *in love* with me, haven't you?'

For one stomach-churning second, Hannah actually thought she might be sick. But it wasn't just the Sheikh's swaggering arrogance which she found so nauseating—it was the way he had said the word *love*. As if it were some unspeakable type of illness. As if it were something beneath his contempt… Clenching and unclenching her fingers, she looked up at him, trying to keep her voice steady. 'What makes you say that?'

'You have been pining for me, I guess,' he said softly, before shrugging his broad shoulders. 'That in itself is not unusual—but the fact that I took your virginity has probably given our night together more significance than it warrants. Am I right, Hannah?'

Hannah flinched, wondering how she could ever have fallen into the arms of someone so unspeakably arrogant.

You know how, whispered the voice of her conscience. *Because he's so irresistible—even now, when he's looking down his haughty nose at you.*

Because despite the insulting reception he'd given her, she was far from immune to the attraction which had got her into all this trouble in the first place.

In Sardinia, she had only ever seen Kulal dressed in western clothes. Faded jeans and T-shirts, impeccably cut business suits or, on that fateful night, a dark dinner suit, just like those worn by all the other men at the party. But today, he was looking emphatically sheikh-like in a robe of white silk which flowed down over his muscular body. A matching headdress, held in place by a circlet of knotted gold, emphasised the stark outlines of his hawk-like features. He looked exotic and powerful. He looked like a stranger. He *was* a stranger, she reminded herself bitterly. A stranger whose child was now living beneath her breast.

'I hate to disillusion you,' she said, concentrating on trying to match his own emotionless tone. 'But I am definitely not pining for you.'

'No? So why come here?' he drawled. 'Why bother flying out here in secret?'

But it hadn't been a secret, had it? His words reminded Hannah that this whole set-up seemed premeditated and that a car had been waiting for her when the plane had touched down. She lifted her chin, the pulsing of a nerve above her jaw the only outward sign of her growing anxiety—because if *Kulal* knew she was here, then who else did? How would such an action appear to the outside world—and, more importantly, to her employers? A lowly chambermaid flying out to confront a desert king! She reflected on her many years of service at the Granchester and a ripple of fear whispered down her spine at the thought of being sacked for such unprofessional behaviour. 'How…how did you know I'd be on that flight?' she questioned croakily.

'Are you really that naïve?' He spat out the question impatiently. 'My security people run automatic checks over all the flight lists and flag up anyone of particular interest and naturally you fell into that category. A woman who needs an urgent visa to visit my country—didn't you consider that might have alerted the suspicions of the authorities?' He gave an impatient sigh. 'Especially since you were asking so many questions about access to the royal palace—and a further check threw up the fact that you work for the Granchester Group and I'd recently been staying in one of their hotels.'

Hannah stared down at her fingernails she'd spent the past few weeks forcing herself not to chew, and suddenly she knew she couldn't put it off any longer. She had to tell him. But it was with an instinctively sinking heart that she met the ebony coldness of his eyes. 'I'm pregnant, Kulal,' she said quietly.

There was a pin-drop silence as he looked at her, the expression on his hawk-like features inscrutable as he shook his head.

'You can't be. I used protection.' His voice was cold. 'I always do.'

Had he added that last bit just to hurt her? To remind her that she was nothing special? Just another women who had succumbed to all that arrogant alpha appeal…? Hannah chewed her bottom lip. Probably. But she wasn't here to protect her own feelings—she was here to do the best for her baby and reacting with anger to his inflammatory comments would serve no useful purpose.

'I'm afraid I can,' she contradicted. 'I'm carrying your baby, Kulal,' she added for extra emphasis and saw his body tense.

Kulal felt the sudden rush of blood to his head as adrenalin flooded through his system and disbelief warred with the evidence right in front of his eyes—because she was here, wasn't she? A place where she had no right to be. He observed her stillness and the unnatural calmness of her expression—as if he was waiting for her to relax and tell him she'd made the whole thing up—but he knew he was waiting in vain. Of *course* she was pregnant—why else would she have flown out here in a dramatic way he suspected was completely out of character? His heart began to pound loudly in his chest and he recognised the sensation instantly because he used to feel that way when he was about to go into battle. But war had never filled him with the uncertainty which now assailed him and which instantly put him on the offensive.

'So have you come here to bargain with me,

Hannah?' he demanded. 'To see how much money you can get out of me?'

Hannah flinched. If she had been in London—if her baby's father had been a *normal* man—she would have risen from the chair, no matter how shaky her legs, and walked out of the room, telling him she would speak to him when he was prepared to be reasonable. Because surely a display of emotion would be justified in those circumstances.

But she wasn't in London and Kulal was *not* a normal man, no matter how much she wished he were. She was stuck in a fancy hotel room in *his* country, miles away from home and everything she knew. The air felt icy from the over-efficient pump of the air-conditioning and outside the huge windows she could see the golden gleam of a beautiful dome. It couldn't have been more unlike the view from her own humble little bedsit, but she mustn't let the undeniable glamour of the location stop her from dealing with practicalities.

'No, I haven't come here to bargain with you,'

she said quietly. 'Nor to be spoken to as if I were someone motivated by nothing other than greed.'

'Really? Then what do you want?'

Wasn't it obvious? Wouldn't anyone with a shred of decency in their soul have done the same—or was Hannah just hypersensitive about the subject of paternity because her own start in life had been less than ideal? She looked into his eyes, but they were cold and hard. As hard as the dagger she'd suddenly noticed was hanging at his hip… 'Because I wanted to give you the opportunity to be a part of your baby's life,' she said quietly.

'In what capacity?'

He was so *cold*. So *unfeeling*. Hannah wanted to pick up a tiny golden box which sat on one of the polished tables. She wanted to hurl it against the wall or the chandelier. To make a noise and to *break* something—as a gesture of defiance as well as one of protest. But she wasn't going to act like a wronged woman—causing a scene and wringing her hands together as she begged him for help. She was going to act with a dignity which would surround her and the baby with a calm and protective aura.

'I hadn't thought that far ahead,' she said. 'I didn't get much further than figuring that you deserved to hear it from me, before anyone else. It's why I came.' She tried and failed to suppress the sudden shiver which made her skin grow all goosebumpy. 'I would have phoned if I could—but, as we both know, you didn't leave a number.'

Kulal nodded, the sudden blanching of her cheeks plucking at his conscience and making him walk towards an inlaid table on which reposed a selection of bottles and glasses. He poured her a long glass of fire-berry cordial and handed it to her, and as their skin touched, the sheer enormity of the life-changing fact once again hit him like a sledgehammer.

She was pregnant.

Pregnant with *his* baby.

Didn't matter that he'd never wanted a child of his own. That he sometimes thought he would prefer his paternal cousin to inherit the kingdom, rather than condemning himself to family life—

a way of life he had always carefully avoided because of the chaos and pain of his own childhood. Even his natural love of independence now took second place, because this changed everything. And he needed to think carefully about what to do next.

Very carefully.

He stared at Hannah, at the fatigue which was creasing the corners of her mouth and the untidy tumble of her hair. 'It's been a long day and you look exhausted, so why don't you go and freshen up?' he suggested.

She put down the half-drunk cordial and as the pink liquid sloshed against the sides of the glass, she regarded him with suspicious eyes. 'What exactly are you suggesting?'

He felt a flicker of irritation. Did she think he was making a pass at her? That he wanted her to go and bathe and prepare herself for him? That he would actually want to be intimate with her at a moment like this, when his whole life was about to change and she was the instrument of that change? *But that wasn't all he felt, was it?*

There was something else. Something he couldn't quite put his finger on. He felt a steely clench around his heart.

Was it fear?

Yet he was known for his fearlessness—even as a teenager, when he'd run away to join the Zahristan forces during the fierce border war with Quzabar. His late father had hit the roof when Kulal returned, with the livid blade mark which travelled from nipple to navel. He had been lucky not to die, the old King had raged—but Kulal hadn't cared about his brush with death. Even before he'd left the palace to fight, he had been given hints of the frailty of human existence. He had learnt lessons which had stayed darkly in his heart. And now it seemed there was another lesson to be learnt.

He stared at her, his lips curling. 'I am merely suggesting you might wish to change—perhaps to rest—before we have dinner.'

She gave a hollow laugh. 'You really think I want to have dinner with you, Kulal?'

'Actually, no. I don't. I think we've been forced

into a position where we're going to have to do things which neither of us will find particularly palatable—'

'I'm keeping my baby!' she defended instantly.

Kulal stiffened, his nostrils narrowing as he inhaled an unsteady breath. 'How dare you imply that I should wish otherwise?' he flared. But although his anger would have filled any of his subjects with fear, it was having no effect on Hannah, for she was tilting her chin in a way which was positively *defiant*.

'I'm just letting you know the ground rules from the start, so there can be no misunderstanding,' she said. 'And I can't see the point of us having dinner.'

'Can't you?' He raised his eyebrows. 'You need to eat and we need to talk. Why not kill two birds with one stone?'

Her gaze became hooded, thick lashes shuttering her aquamarine eyes like dark feathers. 'I feel it's my duty to tell you,' she flared, 'just in case you're getting any autocratic ideas of whisking me away so I'm never heard of again—that my sister knows exactly where I am and she has the number of the police on speed-dial.'

It was such an outrageous remark that Kulal almost smiled until the gravity of the situation hit him and all levity vanished. Because humble Hannah Wilson was not as compliant as he had initially thought, was she?

'Let's say eight o'clock, shall we?' he questioned, eager to reassert his authority. 'And please don't keep me waiting.'

CHAPTER SIX

PRIMED FOR THE Sheikh's knock at precisely eight o'clock, Hannah sneaked one last glance at the mirror, then wished she hadn't. Because this was the reverse side of the fairy tale, wasn't it? This was the reality. Last time she'd spent the evening with Kulal, she had been transformed with a wave of the stylist's magic wand. With her costly jewels and a silken gown she'd looked like someone he might wish to be seen with. But not any more. She had been sick during the early weeks of her pregnancy and, as a consequence, her face had acquired a horrible gauntness. Her dress looked cheap—because it was—her breasts felt heavy, and now she was going to have to endure a stilted dinner in some fancy restaurant with a man who had never wanted to see her again and meanwhile…

Kulal hadn't said a single positive word about the baby.

He hadn't said any of the things she'd secretly been wishing for, even though she'd told herself it was madness to expect anything from such a man. He hadn't reassured her that, although becoming a father had been the last thing on his mind, he would step up to the plate and take responsibility—and he certainly hadn't cooed with pleasure or puffed his chest with pride. He had just studied her dispassionately as if she were no longer a woman, merely an inconvenience who had suddenly appeared in his life. He had installed her in a suite at the Royal Palace Hotel—admittedly the biggest suite she had ever seen. But she had felt small and insignificant within its gilded walls and, when she'd woken from her restless nap, had wandered aimlessly from room to room, wondering what on earth was going to happen next.

An authoritative rap put paid to any further introspection and Hannah opened the door to find Kulal standing there, the bronze shimmer of his robes alerting her to the fact that he too had changed. Had he rushed back to the *real* palace for a quick wash and brush-up, she wondered—just about to tell him that she wasn't sure she could endure going to a stuffy restaurant, when she noticed two hotel employees wheeling a vast trolley towards them, bearing unseen dishes topped with gleaming silver domes.

'I thought we'd eat here,' he said peremptorily, walking into the room without invitation, the waiters trundling the trolley immediately behind him.

Hannah opened her mouth to object to his cavalier attitude then shut it again. Because really, what was the point? While one waiter set the table positioned in a far alcove, she was forced to endure the tops of the silver dishes being triumphantly whipped off by the other, like a magician producing a series of rabbits at the culmination of his act. But she felt no enthusiasm for the feast which was revealed, despite the alluring display of pomegranate-peppered rice and vegetables cooked with nuts and a sweet paste she'd never heard of. She waited until she and Kulal were alone before turning to him, not caring whether her face showed her growing frustration or not.

'Why are we eating here?' she questioned baldly. 'Because you're ashamed of being seen with me?'

He didn't react to her truculent tone, adopting instead a tone of voice she suspected was meant to calm her down.

'A public appearance will serve little purpose other than to aggravate the situation,' he said. 'I don't particularly want reporters seeing us out together—not at this stage. Sit down, Hannah. You should eat something. Now. Before we have any kind of discourse. Before you keel over and faint—because that really *would* be a bore.'

His tone was crisp and authoritative and, although Hannah was still in a mood of rebellion against his high-handedness, she knew that for the sake of her baby she should heed his words. So she sat down opposite him, at a table laid with snowy linen, silver cutlery and crystal glasses—and ate some food with all the enjoyment of somebody being forced to finish a school dinner. It was only when she had put her fork down that she noticed his own plate lay barely touched.

'Yet you aren't eating yourself?' she observed.

'I'm not hungry. I have work to attend to after our meeting and food will make me sleepy.'

His answer left Hannah in no doubt that whatever he was planning, it certainly wasn't seduction—and she was unprepared for the feeling of *rejection* which washed over her. Was he regretting ever having been intimate with her? she wondered. Probably. If she had been in his shoes wouldn't she have felt the same way? Carefully, she folded her napkin—the way she'd seen countless guests do at the Granchester—and placed it on the table. But the first proper meal she'd had in days was actually making her feel stronger—and strength was what she needed right now. Trying not to be affected by the dark glitter of his eyes, she sat back in her chair.

'So,' she said.

'So?' He raised his eyebrows at her questioningly.

Hannah's foster father had been a gambler and she knew a bit about bargaining. She knew that in a situation like this, where the stakes were high, whoever broke first would lose, and who kept their nerve would win. But she suspected that there weren't going to be any real winners or losers in this situation and, besides, she hadn't come here to make demands of him. She didn't want his money or a title, no matter what he might think. She'd come here to give him her momentous news in person and the rest was up to him. And wasn't there something else? The only positive glimmer in his attitude towards her?

'I suppose I should be grateful you haven't demanded a paternity test,' she said.

He shrugged. 'I thought about it. I spent the hours between our meeting this afternoon and coming here this evening wondering whether I should ask the palace doctor to accompany me and have him test you.'

'But you decided not to?'

His eyes glittered as he acknowledged her challenge. 'I did.'

'Might I ask why?'

He leaned back in his chair to study her. 'I realised that a woman who had waited until she was twenty-five to take her first lover would be unlikely to take two within the space of a few months.'

There was a pause as she summoned up the courage to say it. 'Yet you didn't mention it at the time.'

'Your virginity, you mean?' he probed.

For all her newly acquired bravado, Hannah found herself blushing and, as a distraction, took a sip of the delicious sweet-sharp pink drink which she'd never tasted anywhere else. 'Yes.'

'What was I supposed to do? Exclaim with delirious joy?' His lips curved into a mocking smile. 'Or perhaps you expected me to be angry? To demand why you had waited for so long to have sex, and why you hadn't told me?' He shrugged his broad shoulders and his powerful muscles rippled beneath the bronze silk of his robes. 'My ego would not have allowed me to ask such disingenuous questions and, besides, you are not the first virgin I have bedded.'

Oddly enough, that hurt—even though it infuriated Hannah that it should do. She told herself she shouldn't allow herself to be hurt by a man who had never intended their liaison to be anything other than a one-night stand—and it was certainly not a good idea to start imagining the other women who had sighed with pleasure in his arms. 'Anyway, that's beside the point…' she said, determined not to allow a dangerous wistfulness to creep into their negotiations.

His black gaze lasered into her as her words tailed off. 'Which is?'

'I need to know what kind of involvement you'd like in the baby's life. If any,' she added quickly, because she certainly wasn't going to force him into something he didn't want to do. And you can't force him, she remembered. He's a king. 'To know how we're going to deal with this situation.'

He drifted his fingertip around the rim of his crystal glass before lifting his gaze to hers and his face had assumed an almost cruel expression.

'And what would you like to happen, Hannah?' he questioned softly. 'For me to marry you in a glittering ceremony and make you my Queen—is that your secret dream?'

Hannah didn't react in the way she wanted to. In the way her seething hormones were urging her to. Years of keeping the peace were finally paying dividends so that she was able to produce a calm look in response to his arrogant statement.

'Are you making the assumption that I would say yes to such a proposal?' she questioned coolly.

It gave her an inordinate amount of pleasure to see him looking momentarily wrong-footed. And confused.

'You're trying to tell me you would refuse such an offer?' he demanded.

And suddenly all Hannah's determination to keep calm dissolved beneath his arrogant sense of *certainty*. 'Too right I would,' she said fervently. 'I don't really know you and at this moment, I'm not sure whether I even like you. We both probably want completely different things, so why would I marry you? I've had enough experience to realise that unless two people share a common goal, then marriage can be an out-and-out disaster.'

Kulal grew very still because, uncannily, she was echoing his own thoughts on the subject. He stared across the table at her. Had she guessed about his childhood? Pieced together the deliberately vague facts which were the only ones on record and somehow made sense of them? Stored that knowledge away as a point-scoring weapon to use when the time was right?

He sucked oxygen deep into his lungs. No. His parents' marriage had been a secret to the rest of the world because in those days, the press had not been at liberty to report on rumours and hearsay. And although Kulal was regarded as a modern monarch, he was grateful for those historic restrictions. Even his mother's death had been hushed up in the only way which had been acceptable at the time and if you buried something deep enough, you could guarantee it would never see the light of day. He swallowed, wanting something to distract him from the bitter memories which were darkening his mind, and so he did what for him was unthinkable. He asked Hannah about her past.

'Your parents weren't happy?'

She shook her head. 'No.'

'And where are they now?' he said. 'Are they going to make a dramatic appearance, demanding I do the right thing by you?'

Did she recognise that his questions were a tactical move to focus attention on her, not him? Was that why a shadow crossed her face and why her curvy little body suddenly tensed?

'I didn't have any parents.'

'You must have—'

'Oh, there were two people who *conceived* me,' she said, not appearing to care that she'd interrupted him. 'But I didn't know them. Or rather, I can't remember them.'

This was the point at which Kulal would normally grow bored, and wary. He'd learnt to his cost that the more you allowed a woman to talk about herself, the more it gave a falsely inflated sense of her own importance. But he could see this was different. Hannah was not some lover who would soon be removed from his orbit as diplomatically as possible, once he had taken his fill of her. If he wanted any part of his child's life, then she was going to be around for the long-haul.

His mouth hardened. How ironic that his future was to be inextricably linked to a woman he'd spent a single night with. A woman who could not have been more unsuitable for the task of bearing his heir. Yet their child would carry the genes of both their forebears, he reminded himself—so wasn't it his duty to gather as much information as possible? His mouth hardened with new resolve. Because you never knew when such information might become *useful*.

He stared at her, aware that her defiant mask had slipped—showing a trace of vulnerability which had softened her face. And for some crazy reason, he was reminded of the night he'd spent with her, when her rosy lips had trembled whenever he had kissed her. When she'd shivered with ecstasy as he'd brought her to yet another breathtaking orgasm. When she'd curled up in his arms afterwards and clung to his neck like a little kitten. 'So what happened with your parents?' he questioned, aware that his voice had gentled. 'Do you want to tell me?'

Actually, no. Hannah didn't want that. Not at all. But the only thing worse than telling him would be *not* telling him. He seemed to want to keep their liaison and everything else a secret, but she wasn't naïve enough to think they could do that for ever. If word got out that she had been the Sheikh's lover, then wouldn't people start prying into her background and rooting up all kinds of horrible stuff? She would come over as the victim she had tried so very hard not to be.

So take control of the facts and tell him yourself.

'I was brought up in care,' she said slowly. 'With my sister.'

'Care?' he questioned blankly.

'It's when your parents can't look after you—or if they don't want to.'

'And which category did yours fall into?'

Hannah shrugged. 'I don't really know a lot

about them. Only what I was told when I was old enough to understand. My mother was kicked out by her parents when she was seventeen.' There was a pause before she said it, because she didn't want to say it. If she told him, would he freak out? Worry that his baby was going to inherit some disturbing traits, like addiction? But if he freaked out, then so be it. She couldn't change facts and she mustn't start being afraid of how Kulal might choose to interpret them, just because he was in a position of power. 'She developed a drug habit.'

'Your mother was a junkie?' he exclaimed in horror.

Hannah's lips tightened. It was funny how you could still be loyal to someone who hadn't wanted you. Someone who had broken every rule in the parental handbook. 'She didn't inject,' she said defensively, as if that made everything all right, and she found herself wondering if children were conditioned never to give up hope that one day their parents would love them and cherish them. Her hand moved instinctively to lie on her belly and she saw Kulal watching her closely. 'But she took pretty much everything else which was on offer. My father was a rich student from New York, who enjoyed the same kind of...*pastimes*. The pregnancy wasn't planned—obviously.' Her mouth twisted. 'Apparently, my mother wanted to get married. But then his parents arrived from America, scooped him up and put him into rehab and gave my mother a very large cheque, making it clear that, if she cashed it, they never wanted to see her again.'

'And?' he said, into the silence which followed.

'That's exactly what she did. She took the money and ran.'

'So was that a satisfactory outcome?' he questioned softly.

Hannah shrugged. 'Satisfactory for her, I guess—until she ran out of cash. She started renting an apartment which was way too expensive for someone with limited funds and no employment. But in the circles she mixed in, she was suddenly seen as something of a catch—for as long as the money lasted. And that's when she got pregnant with my sister.'

'You mean, your father came back from America?'

'No, that's not what I mean at all,' she said, giving a hollow laugh. 'My sister and I don't share the same father.'

Thoughtfully, he nodded. 'I see. So you're not full sisters, just half-sisters?'

His words were like punches and Hannah recoiled from them. 'Not just *anything*,' she contradicted, her hand slapping against a heart which was racing like a train. 'Tamsyn and I are as close as any two sisters could be and I would do anything for her, do you understand? *Anything*.'

Again, he nodded. 'Tell me what happened to you both.'

Had he used the word *both* to mollify her—a silent admission that he had underestimated her loyalty to her sister? Hannah didn't know, but she found herself wanting to continue with her story. Was that because she never talked about it? Why would she? Yet she was finding it cathartic to let it all out for once, to tell the father of her child all about her chequered background.

'The local council stepped in and put us in a home and tried to get us fostered out as quickly as possible.' She saw another look of non-comprehension cloud his ebony eyes and it occurred to Hannah that, for all his power and position, Kulal was ignorant about some things. Well, of course he was, she thought. He'd been protected for all his privileged life, hadn't he? He wasn't like her. Thrown to the wolves and left to fend for herself… 'They try to find you a family, who can then foster or adopt you,' she explained.

'Is that what happened to you?'

Hannah shrugged as she reached for her glass and took another sip of the sweet-sharp cordial. Yes, a foster home had been found for her and Tamsyn. All the boxes on the form had been ticked by the social worker in charge of the case and everyone had been satisfied that two neglected little girls had a stable home to go to at last. But it hadn't felt like that. How could she explain to a man like Kulal that something which appeared normal on the outside could be anything but normal when you were inside, living it?

'We had a roof over our heads and beds to sleep in,' she said.

Kulal's eyes narrowed. 'You weren't happy?'

She hesitated. 'Happiness is overrated, don't you think?' she said brightly. 'We waste so much time chasing it and, in my experience, it never lasts. My foster father spent most of his money gambling, or wining and dining whichever woman he happened to be seducing at the time.'

His big body suddenly grew tense and his eyes became so dark it was as if someone had suddenly snuffed out all the light which normally gleamed in their ebony depths. 'I think many people have experience of fathers who like sexual variety,' he ground out.

Hannah blinked. Was he saying something like that had happened to *him*? 'You mean your—?'

'This is your story,' he said roughly. 'Not mine.'

She nodded. 'My foster mother was the kind of woman who just pretended nothing was wrong, even though there was barely enough money for food sometimes. She liked to put on a bit of a show in front of all the neighbours. I was forced to resort to unsavoury methods of making sure Tamsyn and I got fed. Skips containing food thrown out by the supermarkets was my favourite.'

He recoiled in horror. 'So why didn't you tell someone in authority? Ask to be sent to a different home?'

'Because Tamsyn was mixed up and difficult!' she burst out, as all the feelings she'd been bottling up for weeks could no longer be contained. 'She'd had a terrible start in life—far worse than mine—and she acted out on it. Not many people could have coped with her and I knew that if I complained, we would be split up.' She pushed back her chair so that it scraped against the marble floor and rose shakily to her feet. 'And I couldn't bear for us to be split up!'

He rose as soon as she did—moving towards her with his bronze robes shimmering as he gestured towards the chair she had just vacated.

'Please sit down, Hannah. I didn't mean to disturb you with my questions.'

'I don't want to sit down! I want…' Her words faded away and suddenly it was all too much. She had told him far too much. Hannah walked over to the window, blinking back the unwanted tears which had sprung to her eyes as she looked out at the turreted skyline.

'I think I know what you want, Hannah.'

She blinked away the blur of tears as his voice grew closer. She could hear the richly accented inflection which reminded her so vividly of the night she'd spent with him. That unforgettable night, when he'd whispered things in a language she hadn't understood but that hadn't seemed to matter at the time. Because Kulal had made her feel like a woman for the first time in her life. He had taken her in his arms and given her the gift of sexual pleasure. Was that why her skin was automatically reacting to the soft caress of his words, even now? Why the tips of her breasts were growing heavy and she found herself longing for him to cup them again, to circle his thumbs over their nail-hard tips and then to take them in his mouth?

With an effort, she reminded herself it was no good getting aroused at a time like this. Or sentimental. She needed to fight the sudden rush of longing which was welling up inside her. But deep down, she was praying he would pull her into his arms and comfort her. Smooth her head as you would a frightened child. Tell her that everything was going to be all right and he would do everything within his power to make that happen.

But he didn't. He just continued speaking in that same measured tone and Hannah didn't dare turn to face him because she didn't trust her own reaction.

'Do you?' she said woodenly.

'Indeed I do. A solution which could work well for everyone.'

'A solution?' she questioned doubtfully, but her question was definitely tinged with hope as she turned to face him.

'Something which would minimise the damage of this unexpected event.'

Minimise the damage. Those were not the words of someone intent on soothing a troubled heart. Those were fighting words—Hannah instinctively recognised that. Ironing every trace of emotion from her voice, she stared into his ebony eyes. 'What exactly did you have in mind, Kulal?'

Unusually, Kulal hesitated before saying his next words, aware of their impact and their power. But what *other* solution could they reach, in the circumstances? He hadn't wanted to be a father but, since the decision had now been forced upon him, he needed to take control. To do the right thing—as he had spent his whole life doing. The only thing. He met the blinking scrutiny of her gaze with a renewed feeling of resolve. 'You say that your own mother was given a cheque in order to make her life easier and that she squandered that sum by living beyond her means.'

'That's right,' she agreed steadily. 'I did.'

'What if I were to go one step further?' he mused. 'What if I were to guarantee you the kind of sum which would mean you wouldn't "run out" of cash ever again?'

'You're talking about a lot of money,' she said carefully.

'I am,' he agreed, with equal care.

'And what would I have to do in return for such a sum?' she questioned, her voice trembling a little now.

'I think we both know the answer to that, Hannah,' he said, almost gently. 'You do the only sensible thing. Give me the child to be brought up as my heir.'

'G-give you the child?' she echoed.

He nodded. 'In the absence of any other heir, this child could inherit all that I own—my lands, my crown and my kingdom. Let your baby go and I promise to do everything in my power to provide everything he or she needs. They will grow up as a Zahristan royal with all the luxury that entails, not someone who is constantly being dragged between two cultures.' He paused and suddenly his face changed, became a harsh, stark study in light and shade. 'Between two people who are little more than strangers to one another.'

Hannah felt grateful for the anger which had

started to flood through her like a tidal wave, obliterating the trembling emotions which his callous words had provoked. Because anger made you strong. It didn't weaken or debilitate you in the way that pain or fear or desire did. Perhaps if she had been bigger she might have flown at him and slapped her palm against his arrogant face and hit him over and over again. But her blows would be ineffectual, and to attack him physically would be to humiliate herself.

Instead, she drew on all her reserves of inner strength as her well-honed survival mode kicked in, just as it had done so many times before. And suddenly it was easy to look at those cruel lips without remembering what it was like to kiss them. And even easier to find the right note of contempt in her voice as she stared into the fathomless gleam of his black eyes.

'I'm not going to dignify your insulting offer with an answer. I'm going back to England, where I will continue working and raising my child on my own as so many other women do. And you can go to hell, Kulal,' she added bitterly.

CHAPTER SEVEN

'HE DIDN'T SAY *THAT*? Come off it, Hannah—you're exaggerating!'

Hannah shook her head as she stared into her sister's emerald eyes. 'I wish I was, but that's the truth,' she said tiredly.

'He offered to *buy your baby*?'

'He didn't phrase it quite as brutally as that, but that's what it came down to, yes.' Hannah moved her shoulders restlessly. 'Perhaps I shouldn't have told you.'

'Too right you should have told me,' said Tamsyn fiercely. 'I feel like going to the papers and exposing him for the man he really is. It's outrageous. It's barbaric! It's—'

'And if you ever do that,' interrupted Hannah quietly, 'in fact, if you ever discuss this with anyone without my permission—I will never speak to you again.'

Tamsyn shook her head, her rich red curls shimmering all the way down her narrow back. 'I just don't get it. You're being loyal to *him*? King Callous? Someone who doesn't deserve your loyalty?'

'I'm trying to do what is best for the baby,' said Hannah as the kettle whistled out the fact that it had boiled. Reaching up, she took two mugs from the cupboard and dropped a peppermint teabag into each. 'And forming some kind of vendetta against the baby's father is not what I had in mind.'

'So he didn't try to stop you when you told him you were leaving?'

Hannah nodded. 'He did. He backtracked and apologised and told me he should never have said it, but the damage was done as far as I was concerned. I told him I had no intention of changing my mind and was flying back to England as soon as I could fix a flight. And that's when he insisted on putting me on one of his private jets.'

'But you refused, right?'

Hannah picked up the kettle and poured boiling water onto the peppermint teabags. She had *wanted* to refuse and pride had been urging her to do just that, but she'd been emotionally wrung out by everything that had happened and physically exhausted, too. She had started to worry that so much stress would be bad for the baby and the thought of being able to sleep in a proper bed on the Sheikh's plane instead of being cramped in the middle of a row of four had proved too powerful a lure to resist. But she hadn't given him her acceptance until one final streak of defiance had reared its head and she had blurted out a sarcastic question to the black-eyed Sheikh who stood before her.

'But what will people think when they see some unknown English chambermaid using the Sheikh's private jet?'

'I don't care what they think,' he'd ground out. 'I am trying to do what is best.'

Her laugh had been bitter. 'Don't you think it's a little late for that, Kulal?'

She had seen him flinch in response to that particular dig and had tried to enjoy his discomfiture. But it hadn't seemed to work like that. She'd just felt completely wretched. So wretched that she hadn't had the energy to refuse a ride in the limousine that had been waiting on her arrival back in London and had whisked her home in purring luxury. It had felt strange stepping out into the gusty chill of the October evening after her brief exposure to the Zahristan sun, but at once she was back to her small room in the Granchester's staff quarters, she'd finally felt able to rest. She had lain down and slept for a solid twelve hours and had woken with a feeling of resolve before demolishing an enormous breakfast.

She'd convinced herself it was best to keep her dreadful trip to Zahristan quiet, but force of habit had made her text Tamsyn to tell her she was back and when her sister had come rushing round, Hannah had found herself blurting everything out. Because they'd always told each other everything…and because she'd felt as if she would burst if she didn't tell *someone*.

'So how did you leave it with the cold-hearted bastard?' Tamsyn was saying as she sipped the peppermint tea which Hannah had just handed her.

You never entirely relinquished the role of elder sister, Hannah thought as she fixed her sister with another expression of mild reproof. 'Please don't say that. His name is Kulal and I refuse to get into name-calling.'

'But he's—'

'He's probably still reeling from the shock of discovering I'm pregnant—and shock makes people react in all kinds of weird ways.'

'Hannah, why do you always have to be so *kind*?'

'I am not being *kind*,' said Hannah, twisting a strand of her long hair round and round one finger. 'I am trying to be practical. Kulal is the father of my child and even if he never wants to see either of us again, I am not going to bring this baby up to hate him.'

'So you'll lie to your child?' accused Tamsyn bitterly. 'Just like you lied to me?'

Hannah's lips flattened. How the past came back to haunt you when you least expected it! Or when you were least equipped to deal with it. 'I never lied to you, Tamsyn. I just tried to present reality in its least painful form,' she said. 'Just like I'm going to do with this baby. When the subject arises, I will just say that I was swept off my feet by a dashing man—which is true.'

'But words won't pay the bills. How the hell are you going to *manage*, Hannah? Do you really think you can live life as a single mother on a chambermaid's wages?'

'Other women manage.'

'And aren't you forgetting something else? I thought Granchester employees weren't allowed to sleep with the guests. What if somebody finds out?'

Hannah winced at her sister's candour. 'Nobody's going to find out, are they?' she said with a confidence she didn't quite feel as she picked up her mug and sipped from it. But the loud ringing of her phone suddenly broke into the uneasy silence and her heart gave a sudden clench as she glanced down at the number before accepting the call. With a rapidly escalating heartbeat, she listened to the voice at the other end and when she'd cut the connection, she looked into Tamsyn's eyes and tried to keep the tremble of fear from her voice. 'That was HR,' she said unsteadily. 'And they want to see me immediately.'

Kulal knocked on a door which was exactly the same as all the others on both sides of the narrow corridor, unprepared for the tiny redheaded figure who flew at him when it was opened.

'You bastard!' she declared, curling her hands into small fists. 'How dare you?'

He honestly thought she might be about to hit him and was wondering whether to summon the female bodyguard he'd had the presence of mind to bring and who was standing just along the corridor, when he saw Hannah appear behind the redhead.

'Tamsyn,' she said, her voice sounding unnaturally calm. 'That kind of talk isn't going to help.'

The redhead didn't budge. 'Says who?'

'I do. And now I'd like you to go home because I need to talk to Kulal.'

'You think I'm leaving you alone? With *him*?'

For the first time, Kulal spoke, realising who the little spitfire must be. 'And if I give you my word that I have your sister's welfare at heart?'

The redhead tilted her chin to fix him with a spitting emerald gaze which was so unlike the cool blue of Hannah's eyes. 'I wouldn't trust your word just as far as I could throw it and I'm not going anywhere!' she declared.

But several minutes later, after repeated assurances from Hannah that she would ring her once 'he' had gone, Tamsyn Wilson departed with another furious shake of her red curls and Kulal was left alone with Hannah.

He looked at her. Her face was pale and her eyes were angry, but there was a dignity about her, too. Something almost *noble* about her demeanour, which had the peculiar effect of making Kulal want to take her in his arms and cradle her, but instinct told him not to dare. She didn't look particularly surprised to see him—her expression was one of resignation. But there was certainly no pleasure or delight on her face and he wasn't used to being given such a lukewarm reception.

'Hello, Hannah,' he said.

Hannah took her time before answering him.

How strange to see the Sheikh of Zahristan standing on the doorstep of her humble staff quarters despite the fact that today he wasn't dressed in the flowing robes and headdress which had made him look so imperious on their last meeting. His immaculate suit was unashamedly cosmopolitan and only the hard planes of his face and distinctive hawk-like features spoke of his particular royal heritage. Her heart was pounding and although she tried to tell herself that the rapid beat was caused by apprehension, she knew that wasn't entirely true. Because her breasts were tingling and there was a tug, low in her belly, which spoke of feelings which were a long way from anger. How was it possible to feel attracted to someone, when they were trying to treat you like an inconvenient object who needed to be moved out of the way as quickly as possible?

Well, he might be a king and she might be a chambermaid, but he would only walk all over her if she let him. So don't let him. She tilted her chin. 'Why are you here, Kulal?'

His gaze was steady. 'Don't you think we have some business to discuss?'

'I thought we'd said everything which needed saying.'

'Please, Hannah.'

Was it hearing him say a word she suspected he didn't use very often which made her relent? 'You'd better come in,' she said ungraciously, turning her back on him and retreating into the small room.

'Thanks,' he said and followed her inside.

'Please don't thank me, Kulal. It's not something I particularly want to do,' she said, watching as he closed the door. 'I just didn't want to have a difficult confrontation in the corridor, with the other staff listening. Though of course I'm no longer a member of staff,' she added. 'Since I've just been sacked—for which apparently I have *you* to thank.' Some of her coolness began to evaporate.

'Couldn't you accept the fact I'd refused your insulting offer to buy my baby?' she demanded, her voice rising as she thought of her blameless work record besmirched by an arrogant piece of manoeuvring by the Sheikh. 'Did the King decide he had to try to get his own way, no matter what? Was that why you got straight on the phone to the owner of the Granchester, just because he happens to be a *mate of yours*? I can't believe you actually rang Zac Constantinides to tell him you'd had sex with me—the woman in Human Resources was practically shaking with rage!'

'I saw no alternative,' Kulal answered calmly. 'You made it clear your intention to continue working as a chambermaid and there was no way I could allow that to happen.'

'Why not?'

'Why not?' Kulal glanced around the small room with a look of genuine consternation, taking in the cramped dimensions and the institutional red-and-white sign which pointed to the fire escape. 'Because you are carrying my child! A child who will be a prince or princess of Zahristan.

What were you thinking was going to happen, Hannah? That you would carry on making beds and cleaning up after guests until you became too cumbersome to continue? And then what? Perhaps you were planning to bring the royal heir back here and place him or her in a crib while you continued to service the rooms?'

She was grinding her teeth together like a little animal. 'I would have managed,' she said fiercely. 'I have always managed in the past.'

In any other circumstances, Kulal might have coldly drawn her attention to the fact that she was only *just about* managing, but once again instinct told him to tread carefully because he could see the flicker of fear in her eyes, which she was desperately trying to hide. 'When is the baby due?' he questioned, trying to remember the word which Zac's wife, Emma, had used. A word Kulal had said many times before, of course—but never in this particular context. 'Are you… *showing* yet?'

This question seemed to annoy her. 'Not yet. I'm only just over twelve weeks and I could have managed to keep it secret for a few weeks more, if you hadn't blurted it out and…' She stared at him and an exasperated sigh escaped her lips. 'Why have you come here today, Kulal? To gloat?'

'Of course it's not to gloat,' he said impatiently. 'I am here because I want to help you.'

'Funny way you have of showing it. I've already told you I'm not interested in your insulting offer and even if you've come here today to increase your price—*my baby is not for sale*!'

'I haven't. In fact, I've given the matter more deliberation. Perhaps I was a little hasty before.'

Her voice was bitter. 'You don't say?'

'I should have considered all the options before I spoke.' Kulal drew in a deep breath, knowing that what he was about to do was the right thing. The only thing he could do, no matter that it went against everything he'd ever wanted. He tried to smile, but his face felt like a piece of concrete, against which the movement of his mouth barely made an impression. He looked at the tiny woman with the belligerent expression. 'I have decided I will marry you after all,' he said heavily. 'It will be a marriage of duty and of sacrifice on both our parts—for the sake of our baby.'

She was staring at him like someone waiting for the punchline. She narrowed her eyes. 'Is this some kind of joke?'

'Why would I joke about something as serious as offering to make you my Queen?'

'I thought we'd already had this conversation. We both agreed that marriage between two people who don't even like each other is a bad idea.'

It was not the reaction he was expecting and Kulal couldn't quite believe it. He searched her face, wondering if it was a feigned response designed to make him push his case more strongly, but her consternation seemed genuine. Surely she was not opposed to a proposition which most women would have leapt at? He studied her more closely. The sharp pallor which had been in evidence when she had flown to Zahristan had given way to a healthy glow, against which her eyes sparkled like pale blue stars. The pregnancy had made her dark hair even more lustrous than before and it hung in gleaming waves around her shoulders. Perhaps it was time to take charge. To show her he had strength enough for both of them. And wouldn't action be more effective than words—reminding her that they had a rare chemistry between them?

Closing the small space between them, he reached out and pulled her into his arms, recognising from her instinctive shiver of pleasure that sometimes a woman could crave a man's touch, even if she didn't want to. He ran his thumb down the side of her cheek, giving her time to move away, because no way would he be accused of coercion. But she didn't move. She stayed right where she was and her mouth was trembling with unspoken invitation as he lowered his head towards hers.

Their lips collided—first hard, then soft.

A meeting and then a slow exploration.

He heard her moan and the sound was enough to fuel his rising need. Barely a whisper of breath passed from her mouth into his—but it contained a hunger which mirrored his own. His arms tightened and he could feel her breasts pressing into him, her nipples hardening like tiny bullets against his chest. And Kulal found himself driven on by an urgent hunger because never had a kiss tasted as sweet as this. As sweet as any battle victory, he thought longingly, as his tongue laced with hers. Was it because she was pregnant with his child, or because she was the only woman who had ever opposed him and that in itself was a huge turn-on?

'Hannah,' he husked out, aware of the rocky hardness between his thighs and longing to lose himself deep inside her. 'Be my bride.'

Afterwards, he would curse himself for having spoken because his words shattered the erotic interlude—more than that, his momentary sexual hunger had given *her* all the power. Suddenly, the spell was broken and she pulled away from him, her eyes blazing. She swayed a little and automatically, he put out his hand to steady her, but she waved him away.

'Are you out of your mind?' she demanded, untidy locks of hair tumbling around her flushed cheeks. 'Coming onto me like that when we're supposed to be having a discussion about our baby?'

'Are you trying to deny that you wanted me?' he mocked.

She shook her head. 'No. I can't deny that, but it was…inappropriate. Just like your proposal of marriage was inappropriate.'

'Why?' he demanded hotly.

'Do you think I'm a fool, Kulal? That just because I make beds and clean rooms for a living, I'm incapable of understanding what's staring me in the face?'

Momentarily wrong-footed by such a mercurial switch of mood, Kulal narrowed his eyes. 'I make no such judgment of your character.'

'Are you sure? Did your advisors tell you to marry me after your initial aversion to the idea? Did they suggest that if I wasn't prepared to sell you my baby, then a king's ring on my finger would mean you could get hold of your child by legal means instead?'

'You think that I would take such advice from my *advisors*?' he thundered. 'They would not dare presume to tell me how to live my life!' He drew in a deep breath. 'The decision is mine and mine alone—and besides, marriage to me would protect you, not weaken you.'

She shook her head. 'No, it wouldn't. It would simply make me your possession. We both know that.'

Frustratedly, Kulal turned away from her, staring out of the tiny window which overlooked a courtyard, in which plastic bins were lined up like sentries. Rain had begun to slant down in a thin grey curtain. Everything looked so grey, he thought, and as he tried to imagine his child growing up in such an environment, a feeling of powerlessness washed over him. Once, he had vowed never to allow himself to feel that way again, but suddenly he recognised that you couldn't always dictate events. That sometimes life took you along a path you hadn't intended, and having a royal status made no difference to that journey. He had grown up with all the riches in the world, but that hadn't made a bit of difference to the fact that he and his brother had been at the mercy of a manipulative mother who had wanted only one thing. And it hadn't been them.

His mouth hardened. His mistrust of the opposite sex was rooted deep in his psyche and Hannah Wilson was reinforcing all his worst prejudices. He knew only too well how unpredictable women could be and here was a prime example of someone who manifested that dangerous, innate quality. It hadn't taken long for the humble chambermaid to morph into a self-possessed creature who was airily rejecting a king's marriage proposal, had it? She was far less of a pushover than she should have been, given her status. Did the knowledge that his flesh grew inside her give her the confidence to address him as if he were any other man?

He was tempted to tell her that she would obey him because his wishes were always acceded to. Yet he recognised it wasn't that simple. He couldn't *force* this Englishwoman to marry him, but maybe he could persuade her.

Once again, he allowed his gaze to linger on the cramped dimensions of the tiny staff room. 'So where are you planning to live, once you leave your job?'

Hannah had thought about this. A lot. She hated the fact that economically, she and Kulal were poles apart, but there wasn't a lot she could do about it. She thought longingly about money she'd saved. Money which had taken so long to accumulate and which was nearly enough for the deposit on a tiny apartment. It didn't look as if that little dream of independence was going to happen now, but sometimes you had to let your dreams go. 'I have savings I can live on.'

'How long do you think they're going to last?'

She shrugged. 'Long enough. And when they run out, I can find myself a job as a housekeeper—somewhere which will provide a roof over my head for me and my baby.'

'A housekeeper?' he exclaimed in horror. 'You think I would ever allow you to bring up the future prince or princess of Zahristan as the child of a *housekeeper*?'

'But you can't…' Her fingers moved to her

neck, spreading wide as if to disguise the flickering pulse there. 'You can't stop me.'

'You don't think so?' He gave a cynical laugh. 'I can certainly try. I can assign bodyguards and have you watched twenty-four-seven. Every move you make will be reported back to me and analysed.' His eyes were dark. Dark as the coal at the bottom of a bunker which had never seen daylight. 'And before you protest that such a move would be invasive—let's just say I am protecting what is mine.'

'The courts will ask you to pay maintenance.' There was raw appeal in her voice now. 'And I'm not too stupid or too proud to turn it down. Surely that's enough to reassure you that the baby and I won't be living in poverty.'

'Yes, I will pay maintenance,' he affirmed coldly. 'I don't need a court of law to make me honour my obligations. But my child will not have the life it is owed by royal blood. By turning down my offer of marriage, you are condemning he or she to a life of illegitimacy. Is that really what you want, Hannah?'

Hannah flinched as Kulal's words pierced through her armour at last. Having worked his way through all other arguments, had he saved the most powerful for last? Oh, *why* had she told him about her sordid past? Had she really been naïve enough to think he wouldn't store up that information and use it against her if needed? Because her illegitimacy—and Tamsyn's—had always been the dull pain which had eaten away inside her. The shame which had provided the backdrop to their young lives. It had emphasised Hannah's feelings of insecurity and although she'd pretended not to care about being born out of wedlock, she *had* cared. Things were different these days and nobody seemed to care very much whether a man and a woman went through a marriage ceremony before having a child, but it hadn't always been that way.

And she was not carrying any child.

This was a *royal child.*

The flat of her hand drifted down to touch her belly, like someone touching wood for luck—but somehow Hannah sensed that there was no *luck* to be found. 'I could run away and you could never find me,' she breathed.

'I would find you,' he said.

He was beating down her arguments, one by one, and Hannah's head was spinning as she tried to imagine what marriage to such a man would mean. A few minutes ago, he had taken her in his arms and kissed her and she had let him. She had done much more than let him—and he was experienced enough to realise how much she wanted him. She might have had the presence of mind to pull away, but what if he approached her during one of those vulnerable moments which seemed to be on the increase? What then?

Did she really imagine that a man like Kulal would be content to live a celibate life with his new bride?

Lifting her gaze to his, she tried to keep her voice matter-of-fact, but she could feel colour creeping into her cheeks as she asked the all-important question. 'If I were to agree to this…*marriage.*' She drew in a deep breath. 'Do you mean a marriage in…in every sense of the word?'

He seemed to find her discomfiture amusing. 'There's no need to look so terrified, Hannah—I won't be chaining you to the bed and demanding my conjugal rights. Unless that's your secret fantasy, of course.' He gave the ghost of a smile. 'The purpose of marriage is procreation and since we've achieved that without really trying, that just leaves sex. And we're both adults. We both need that release. In fact, I think the sex could work very well between us, since neither of us are blinded by emotion.'

'I can't…' She shook her head, shocked by the matter-of-fact way he had just come out and spoken about *release*. As if they were nothing but a pair of rutting animals. 'I can't think about that right now. It's all such a lot to take in.'

'Indeed it is. For both of us.' His gaze grew thoughtful. 'And you still haven't given me your answer.'

Hannah stared at him, knowing there was only one answer she could give him. Because she didn't have the energy or the inclination to spend her life fighting all that royal power and might, not when she suspected that, ultimately, Kulal would win. 'I will marry you, yes—to make our baby legitimate.'

'Good.'

'And if we find living together intolerable—what then?'

'If we agree from the outset not to make unrealistic demands on each other, then I see no reason why we should find it intolerable.'

'What kind of…unrealistic demands are you talking about?'

His face darkened, his hawk-like features tautening into a forbidding mask. 'I'm talking about love,' he said harshly. 'I don't ever want your *love*, Hannah. Do you understand?'

He said the word as if he had just sworn. As if it were a curse. And Hannah couldn't decide whether to commend him for his honesty or chastise him for his arrogance. Did he just assume that every woman would end up falling in love with him, no matter how badly he treated them? 'I don't think there's any danger of that, Kulal,' she said. 'But if we can't make it work…' she met the gleam of his eyes and said what needed to be said '…then I want your word that you will grant me my freedom and let me return to England.'

Kulal felt a wave of pity as she looked at him, but he didn't comment. Did she *really* think he would ever allow her to take his child out of the country? That he would meekly grant her the divorce she would no doubt demand? Shoving his hands deep into the pockets of his trousers, he clenched his fists. He had never imagined he could feel this way about something which didn't even exist, but when he thought about his unborn baby, something fierce licked at the solid ice which had always surrounded his heart. Fatherhood had been thrust upon him without warning and his response to it had taken him by surprise. Because he wanted this child, he realised. Wanted it with a fervour he had never known before.

And this woman would not stand in his way.

'We don't have to think about that right now,' he said silkily. 'Let's just get through the wedding, shall we?'

CHAPTER EIGHT

THE IMAGE WHICH stared back at her was strange and Hannah had never seen anything quite like it before. A woman clad entirely in a golden gown, the soft gleam emphasising the four-month curve of her fecund belly. The metallic shimmer looked more like armour than satin and her floaty veil of golden thread was held in place by a coronet of bright diamonds, which were fashioned to look like flowers.

This is me, thought Hannah—except it doesn't look like me.

This was the last time she would stand in front of a mirror as a single woman. A last glimpse of the old Hannah, before she was taken into the vast throne room where Kulal and the rest of the wedding party were waiting for her so the ceremony could begin. And *what* a wedding party.

A nervous shiver ran down her spine because the size of the congregation was daunting—more than that, all the guests seemed to be billionaires or royalty.

Hannah reminded herself that she'd worked for these kinds of people ever since she'd been a rookie sixteen-year-old starting at the Granchester, and they were only flesh and blood—just like her. Even so, she didn't usually *socialise* with political leaders and sultans or academics and sports stars. The only person she'd met before was Salvatore Di Luca, who had arrived at the palace the previous evening and greeted her with a warmth which felt manufactured. She wondered if he remembered her as the last-minute guest Kulal had taken to his fancy party and whether he secretly disapproved of their unlikely union.

At least Zac Constantinides and his wife, Emma, had been unable to attend, and Hannah had felt nothing but relief when they'd cited a prior engagement in Zac's native Greece. Imagine how embarrassing *that* would have been—saying her vows in front of the ex-boss who'd been forced to fire her. It was just unfortunate that his cousin Xan was present and that he and Tamsyn seemed to have had some kind of run-in during the rehearsal last night.

She pleated her lips together as she made a final unnecessary adjustment to her veil, terrified Tamsyn was going to cause some kind of scene today. Because her little sister was on the rampage and making no attempt to hide her displeasure. Had Tamsyn guessed she was being railroaded into this marriage, despite her repeated assurances to the contrary? And was she determined to fight Hannah's corner for her, as her big sister had done for her so many times in the past?

But in the end, the choice Hannah had been forced to make had been a no-brainer.

Marriage which would confer legitimacy on her unborn child.

Or life as a struggling singleton, with the ever-present fear that Kulal might use his power and his influence to snatch her offspring away from her.

The soft voice of one of the servants interrupted

Hannah's reverie with a gentle question. 'You are ready, mistress?'

Hannah nodded as she picked up the heavy spray of white hyacinth interwoven with juniper berries—both national flowers of Zahristan. Briefly, she lifted the blooms to her nostrils, closing her eyes as she inhaled the heady scent—and then the ornate double doors were opened and she walked into the crowded throne room.

Hannah was aware of all eyes turning in her direction, but her self-consciousness dissolved the moment Kulal stepped towards her. Was it the fact that his eyes gleamed with what looked like approval, or was it the touch of his warm flesh as he brushed his hand over her cold fingers? Because in that moment, everyone else in the high-ceilinged chamber seemed to fade away as she focused her gaze on the man who would soon be her husband.

Beneath her wedding dress, she felt the tight squeeze of her heart—for this was Kulal as she'd never seen him before, wearing the richly embellished robes he'd told her were traditional for a marrying sheikh. He looked so tall and formidable, his raven hair covered by a shimmering headdress and his hawk-like features set and tense. Against the olive gleam of his skin, his eyes were like black diamonds, but as she studied him more closely, Hannah wondered if she had imagined the pain which had briefly shadowed their depths.

Was this ceremony bringing back memories she suspected he kept locked away? He'd told her that all Zahristan kings married within the walls of this ornate room, which meant that his parents must have made their vows here. Was he thinking of them now? Wishing they'd been here to witness the occasion? She'd asked him about his family last night, but his answers had been spare and unwilling, imparting only the most basic of facts. His parents were both dead, and he hadn't seen his twin brother for many years. She'd started to ask why, but he had shut down her queries, telling her that the rehearsal was about to begin.

As she stepped towards the velvet-covered kneeling stool, Hannah was aware of how little she knew about her future husband, but perhaps it was better this way. If she knew the answers, mightn't she get freaked out by the enormity of what she was about to do?

'You are ready?' he said softly.

She nodded, wondering how many more people were going to ask her that. Were they giving her a final opportunity to change her mind? To take her chances and go at it alone? But the time for that had passed. There was no point looking back and thinking about all the 'might have beens'. Didn't matter what had brought them to this moment—what mattered was how they dealt with it. She should be grateful that her child would never have to go hungry, as she had done. Or have to lie in bed at night, fearing eviction because the rent hadn't been paid. Glad, too, that they would bear the name of their father.

Hannah had always made the best of whatever situation she'd been in, so why not continue doing that now? Kulal had warned her not to love him, but there were plenty of workable alternatives to love. Couldn't she learn to respect and to care for him, so that they could be decent parents to their child and something approaching friends to each other? Looking up into the glitter of the Sheikh's eyes, she nodded.

'I'm ready,' she said and smiled.

Kulal tensed as the look she slanted him made his heart kick. Today she seemed receptive, whereas last night at the rehearsal, she had seemed anxious. Glancing around and asking him questions he'd felt unable to deal with, when he was trying to organise one of the most spectacular weddings this desert region had seen in a decade. He could have opted for a more intimate service—some pared-down celebration which could be followed by a lavish party. But something inside him had baulked at that. He didn't want something *hushed up.* Something which would carry echoes of the secrets and senselessness of the past.

Was that the reason why he had evaded Hannah's guileless queries about his late parents? Why he had mentioned his twin brother only in passing? Because what was the point in her knowing stuff—dark stuff—which might affect the way she viewed life here at the palace?

But his heart still clenched as he acknowledged the empty space where his brother should have stood, on the opposite side of the gilded throne room. The runaway twin who had left his desert home at the earliest opportunity, never to return. His no-show today had come as no real surprise, though Kulal couldn't deny the dull beat of disappointment. Had Haydar been shocked at his twin's sudden decision to take a bride—a move which had been made clear when Kulal had confided that Hannah was pregnant? He had wondered whether the baby news would take some of the pressure off his brother, would make him forget about the unbearable reality of their own upbringing. Yet he had not succeeded and it seemed Haydar was determined to continue with his self-imposed exile from his homeland.

But Kulal would not think of that today. He would think only of a duty which had been forced upon him and which he must now make the best of.

He stared down at the top of Hannah's head and the fine golden mesh which covered her shiny hair. In England, she had hinted that theirs might be a marriage in name only—but that was something he refused to countenance. Their union *would* be consummated, he decided grimly, because a satisfied woman was a compliant woman. He would keep her sweet until their child was born.

And after that, she could do whatever the hell she wanted.

He spoke his vows without emotion, hearing Hannah repeat hers through the English interpreter which had been provided by her embassy. He felt her hand tremble as he slid the gold and ruby ring on her finger and turned her huge aquamarine eyes to his.

'You are now my wife,' he said, and as the interpreter translated his words into English the entire international congregation broke into spontaneous applause. He saw the way her teeth slid into her bottom lip, in that way women sometimes had of expressing pleasure. Was she revelling in the fact that she now wore a priceless wedding band and people were bowing and curtseying to her? Was this marriage what she had wanted all along—and all that hesitation false? 'Happy?' he questioned, aware of people around them listening and feeling it his duty to echo the usual sentiments of the bridegroom.

Looking up into Kulal's black eyes, Hannah didn't want to answer. She suspected he hadn't forgotten the bright assertion she'd made that happiness was overrated—just as she suspected he had only asked the question because there were lots of people milling around them. But then he lifted her fingers to his lips and kissed them, his gaze not leaving her face, and in that moment the truth became blurred. She felt a familiar warmth rush through her veins and, beneath the heavy gold dress, her nipples tightened. And suddenly it was easier to focus on the cravings of her body rather than the emptiness in her heart. If she concentrated on desire, which was starting to lick over her skin like a low-grade fever, rather than the fact that Kulal didn't care for her, wasn't it almost possible to feel the thing she didn't really believe in?

'Very happy,' she said.

His hawk-like features hardened and his eyes darkened. He moved his hand to her waist, his thumb softly stroking at the metallic indentation before propelling her towards a gilded anteroom, where silent servants were circulating with trays of drinks. 'Then let's do what we need to do,' he said roughly. 'Let's play out this pantomime to the full until I can get you alone.'

Hannah's throat was dry with sudden nerves as she was introduced to guest after stellar guest, but it wasn't social unease which was making her feel jittery. It was the unmistakable message of sexual intent which glittered from Kulal's black eyes whenever he looked at her—which was a *lot*. Had she really been naïve enough to think that theirs might be a marriage in name only? She found herself wondering if it was obvious to everyone else that the desert King was looking on his new bride with unashamed lust.

And that she was feeling exactly the same way about him.

The wedding feast took place in an enormous dining gallery, with musicians playing a kind of dreamy music she'd never heard before. One elaborate course followed another—so many that Hannah lost count. But she only picked at the delicious fare, because her weighty golden gown didn't exactly provide a lot of room for expansion. Nobody had actually *mentioned* her pregnancy—she supposed nobody would dare—but it must have been obvious to anyone, especially to the Zahristan dressmaker who had been dispatched to London to make her wedding gown.

Following a fulsome speech from the country's Prime Minister and then a few heavily edited anecdotes from Salvatore, she and Kulal stood up to raise their jewel-encrusted goblets in a toast, before entwining arms so that they could drink from each other's cup. Afterwards, Kulal clasped her fingers in his and led her onto the dance floor. But this was nothing like the private dance they'd shared in Sardinia when they'd been watched by nothing but the silver moon. Now she felt like an exhibit in the zoo as all the guests circled to watch their shimmering movements. Were they observing her bulky silhouette? She was just sixteen weeks pregnant, but her tiny stature made her look much further ahead in her pregnancy than she really was.

And all the longing which had been building up inside her began to evaporate beneath the spotlight of the spectators' stares. Perhaps they were thinking that Kulal had fallen for the oldest trick in the book—though they'd probably be even more appalled if they realised that theirs had been a one-night relationship. Looking around in vain for the encouraging smile of her sister, Hannah felt like a mannequin in her new husband's arms. She was relieved when finally he led her from the vaulted gallery, past the bowing servants who lined the corridors as they made their way towards Kulal's private rooms. Hers, too, from now on, she reminded herself grimly.

But for how long?

As he gestured her inside, Hannah looked

around. She'd only been in the palace for a week—which had been spent in her own lavish quarters on the other side of the palace. She had been more than comfortable there, close to the palace's vast central courtyard, where peacocks wandered amid orange trees and the air was fragrant with the heady perfume of gardenia. Kulal had given her a guided tour of all the state rooms, as well as the dimly lit library with all its ancient books, and she remembered her momentary burst of pleasure as she'd realised that here were all the tools to continue her learning. He had shown her the throne room and the crown jewels—to which she would have unfettered access as his new bride. After that, he had taken her to the state-of-the-art stables, as well as the garage complex with a fleet of cars which could have graced any international Grand Prix circuit.

But nothing could compete with the splendour of the King's private residence with its soaring pillars and gilded rooms which each flowed seamlessly into the next. Low velvet divans were scattered with brocade cushions and faded silk rugs were strewn over the floors. Intricate silver lanterns hung from the vaulted gleam of the golden ceiling and the air was richly scented with incense.

'You look subdued, Hannah,' Kulal observed softly as the massive doors clanged shut behind them, leaving them alone at last. 'Does the thought of your wedding night fill you with trepidation?'

She met his ebony gaze and remembered what it had been like when she'd used to clean for him in Sardinia, when her days had seemed impossibly simple and free from care compared to now. When he'd shown her his country on the map and talked about mountains and rivers and the rare, pink-tinted Zahristan deer which drank at the crystal streams, and which you could sometimes observe if you were very quiet. Sometimes he would actually ask her opinion about something and his eyes used to gleam with humour when she told it the way it really was. When she'd talked to him as if he were just a normal man, rather than a royal potentate. Couldn't she do that now?

'I'm scared I'm going to get lost among all these marble corridors,' she admitted.

A brief smile played on his lips but, visibly, he seemed to relax. 'And that's all?'

No, of course it wasn't all. She was terrified of the wedding night which lay ahead, despite the desire which was never far from the surface. Terrified that her newly bulky shape would kill his passion for her stone-dead. And there were other fears, too—nebulous things she didn't dare acknowledge, especially not in these nervous moments before the Sheikh claimed her as she knew he would.

But she had vowed to try to make this marriage work, hadn't she? To give it her best shot—and she wouldn't be able to do that if she behaved like a chambermaid. She could only succeed in her role as his desert Queen if she adopted a new confidence—if she started believing in herself and her ability to make this work, as she had done so many times before.

Sucking in a deep breath, she lifted the diamond coronet and the golden veil from her head and carefully set them down on a nearby table and began to walk towards him. Each step felt as if it were covering an infinite amount of space during a short journey which seemed to take for ever. And then she was standing before him, her eyes fixed firmly on his, praying that he would be the master of what happened next because, although she was trying like mad to believe in herself, she didn't think she was up to seducing the Sheikh in such intimidating surroundings.

'Not quite all,' she admitted in a rush. 'I feel nervous about the night ahead even though I have no right to. I mean, it's not like I'm a virgin any more, and—'

He silenced her, not with his kiss but with a forefinger placed over her lips. 'You have every right to feel nervous,' he said gravely. 'For although you are no longer a virgin, you are still relatively inexperienced and today must have been very difficult for you in many ways.'

She nodded, warmed enough by his consideration to confide her biggest fear. 'It was pretty daunting,' she confessed. 'And it wasn't helped by wondering where Tamsyn had got to.'

'Or Xan Constantinides,' he offered drily. 'He left the ballroom soon after her. Didn't you see them go?'

'No, I didn't.' Hannah bit her lip. 'Isn't he supposed to be a terrible womaniser?'

'I'm afraid so.'

'Do you think she's okay?'

'I'm sure she's physically safe, if that's what you mean—though it's probably inadvisable to sleep with Xan Constantinides unless she's prepared to get her heart broken.'

'That's the last thing she needs right now!' said Hannah urgently. 'Kulal, we've got to find her!'

He raised his eyebrows. 'What do you want me to do—spend my wedding night ordering my guards to extricate Constantinides from her clutches?'

'Or her from his!' she declared loyally.

Kulal frowned. 'Tamsyn is an adult, Hannah—just like you. I'm sure you were the exemplary big sister to her when you were growing up, but don't you think it's time you cut the apron strings?'

She'd thought that plenty of times, but habit was one of the hardest things to break. 'I don't think it's a good idea if she starts associating with people who are way out of her league,' she said, meeting the sudden mockery in Kulal's eyes.

'Like you did, you mean?'

She was trying to think of a suitable response when suddenly the Sheikh seemed to lose patience with the conversation because he picked her up.

'What are you doing?'

'What do you think I'm doing? I'm taking you to bed. I've had enough talking, particularly about your sister.'

He began to carry her towards a beautiful carved arch at the far end of the room and Hannah kicked her legs a little like a toddler learning to swim.

'Please put me down, Kulal. I'm much too heavy.'

'You weigh nothing,' he said, carelessly discounting her protest. 'Nothing at all.'

And perhaps he decided that kisses *were* better than words—for kisses took you down one path and words another. Perhaps he was bored with talking altogether, for he set her down beside the biggest bed she'd ever seen and pulled her into his arms.

CHAPTER NINE

'SO,' SAID KULAL, his voice unsteady. 'Time to seduce my new wife. But first, I need to get you out of this infernal wedding dress.'

Hannah's heart was hammering as the Sheikh turned her round to begin unhooking her decorative gown. It seemed to take him ages, but that might have had something to do with the fact that he kept brushing his mouth over each inch of newly exposed flesh, so that by the time he had laid her trembling and naked beneath the embroidered bedcover, all her nerves had dissolved beneath a feeling of mounting anticipation. Just *enjoy* this, she told herself fiercely as he pulled the ceremonial robes from his darkly muscular body and slid naked into bed beside her. Because this is your wedding night and it will lay the foundations of your whole life together.

'I've never had sex with a pregnant woman before,' he murmured as he grazed his mouth over hers.

Brushing the back of her hand across her forehead, Hannah mimed relief. 'Thank goodness for that.'

He paused, lifting his head away from hers so that their gazes collided. 'I don't want to hurt you, Hannah.'

'I'm tough,' she said truthfully, though she was talking physically, not emotionally. Because when he looked at her in that seeking way, she felt almost boneless with a deep longing which was alien to her. But surely she was permitted to experience it on her wedding night… Surely just this once she could hint at all the passion lying deep inside her, waiting to be unlocked. 'Just hold me, Kulal.' Her voice trembled a little. 'Touch me.'

His features hardened as he stared at her and she wondered if she'd sounded needy. But suddenly, his mouth was on hers and he was kissing her with a hunger which seemed to echo her own and she felt a great whoosh of excitement flooding through her. And although Hannah wasn't—in Kulal's own words—very experienced, somehow that didn't seem to matter. Not to her and not to him. Not now, when she was his wife. When she was at liberty to touch him without inhibition. And why be shy when his baby was in her belly? Wasn't their flesh combined in more than one way?

'Oh,' she said breathlessly as he began to drift his fingertips over her skin.

'Your breasts are magnificent,' he said throatily.

'You don't think they're too…big?'

He gave a strangled kind of laugh. 'What kind of a question is that?'

Now wasn't the time to admit that the fashion magazines which Tamsyn had always passed on to her to read had always made Hannah feel like an over-curvy freak. Not when he was bending his head to suck hotly on each aroused nipple. She shivered as his fingertips skated over the curve of her belly, lingering there for just a moment. She waited for him to say something about the baby, but he didn't and she told herself it was stupid to feel disappointed. To think that if this were a *normal* honeymoon, then he might have mentioned the unborn life within her.

But why think about the things he wasn't saying when his seeking fingers were delving in between her parted thighs and beginning to stroke her. He was tantalising her as he rubbed his fingers against her slick, wet heat until she moved restlessly—her hunger beginning to mount.

She knew she couldn't just lie there passively. During her solitary nights last week on the other side of the palace, she'd furtively read a book on sexual satisfaction within marriage, which she planned to put to good use. But when she summoned up the courage to slide her palm over the enormous erection which was nudging hard against her belly, Kulal dragged his mouth away from hers and gave a decisive shake of his head, before moving her hand away.

'No,' he said sternly.

'Why not?'

'Because I'm too close to coming and I want to do that when I'm inside you.' His voice was almost gentle as she sank her hot face into the sanctuary of his neck. 'And I don't really think that now is the time for blushes, Hannah. Do you?'

She remembered that once he'd told her he liked her blushes, but that had been way back when—when he'd thought she would be in and out of his life in a few short hours. If he had been able to look into the future—if he'd known that their single night in Sardinia would have ended with her as his new Queen in this amazing golden palace—would he still have gone ahead and had sex with her?

Of course he wouldn't.

Would she?

But the crazy thing was that Hannah couldn't find herself regretting that night—and not just because Kulal had introduced her to a physical pleasure she was discovering hadn't been a one-off. It was more than that. Because already she felt a fierce love for the new life growing inside her—so how could she possibly have regrets?

'Hannah,' he said sternly, as if he'd guessed she was miles away. 'Pay attention.'

With a shy smile, she opened her mouth to his and that was when sensation took over, obliterating all thought and replacing it with feeling. She swallowed as his moist tip nudged against her and gasped as he eased himself inside her molten heat.

'No protection,' he exclaimed as he stilled inside her and gave an exultant sigh. 'Just you and me, with nothing in between us.'

She knew his words were supposed to be erotic, but Hannah felt deeply emotional as he filled her with his hard length and began to move. She'd wondered if making love while she was pregnant would feel any different, but the blissful truth was that it felt amazing. Maybe even better than that blissful night in Sardinia. It certainly felt more *intimate*. Almost *too* intimate. She clung to him as his thrusts deepened and she felt the tantalising build of orgasm, but she was so intent on kissing him that it seemed to creep up on her by stealth, so that when pleasure came, she cried out his name in a way she hadn't planned, the gasped word echoing around the vast bedchamber so that it sounded like some sort of *prayer*.

Was she imagining the sudden tension in his body before his movements resumed and he shuddered out his own release?

Afterwards, she waited for him to say something, because she had no idea about post-sex protocol, especially between a man and a woman who'd been forced to marry. Did they act as if today had been no big deal? Did she try to explain that the curiously vulnerable way she'd called out his name hadn't actually *meant* anything? She waited for some sort of reassuring hug, but instead he rolled away from her, his hot black gaze briefly roving over her rounded curves, before lying on his back, his breathing still ragged.

'So…' She cleared her throat. 'All in all, I thought today went off quite well, didn't you?'

He could hear the faltering delivery of her words and a battery of responses ran through Kulal's mind, but he took his time before selecting one. Should he tell her he'd felt nothing but duty as he had exchanged those meaningless vows? Yet the truth was that he'd been almost *comfortable* with that, because he was familiar with detachment and he enjoyed the barrier it created between him and the rest of the world. That part had all gone according to plan and afterwards, at the reception, he had acknowledged the congratulations offered by the Sheikhs and Sultans of adjoining regions, knowing that his royal line would be continued. Again, so far, so expected.

But when he had brought his new wife to bed…

He swallowed.

When he had stripped away her constricting bridal gown to reveal the cushioned flesh which had burgeoned so much since last time he'd seen it and which had welcomed him so eagerly, he hadn't felt quite so detached then, had he? He told himself it was because he'd never had unprotected sex with a woman before and that was the reason why it had felt so…

He stared at the dappled rose light which flickered across the ceiling.

So what?

As if he'd never been that close to a woman before—which in one sense was true, because he'd never had sex without the obligatory thin layer of latex. Was that the reason why he had felt so alive and so *vital*? Why his heart was still pounding fit to burst in his chest? It had been the most incredible sexual experience of his life, yet he couldn't deny that his response had the potential to add complications to his life. Especially if Hannah got the wrong idea. He didn't want his new bride to think his rapturous reaction meant anything more than an amazing orgasm.

Because that was all it had been.

All it ever could be.

Kulal stifled a sigh. Once he had found out about her pregnancy, he'd been determined to keep his baby and known it would make more sense if Hannah was around, too. It would certainly make it easier. But while he was prepared to be *reasonable* to get her to stay, he would not lie to her. Because lies could seep into people's lives like poison. They could darken everything they touched. And the first lie was always the most dangerous. The gentle tap which would send the whole line of dominoes tumbling down…

'Not as bad as I expected,' he said, turning his

head to look at her. 'I think it served its purpose, don't you?'

'Oh.'

Her voice sounded muffled and he didn't have to see her face crumple to sense her disappointment. That much was evident from the sudden slump of her shoulders and the way she'd started chewing her lip. Was she secretly longing for him to adorn the day with romantic embellishments which didn't exist? Or was she trying to guilt-trip him—even though she'd known the score from the very start?

'What did you want me to say, Hannah?' he demanded. 'That it was the most wonderful day of my life?'

'No, of course not.'

He saw the confusion which had clouded her eyes and fury at being hit by another wave of guilt prompted his next words. 'To go through a marriage I didn't particularly want—you think that gives me pleasure?'

His words were harsh but honest, and he thought she might turn away from him. To lie there trembling with silent resentment. And wasn't that what he wanted her to do? To draw a line in the sand between them that she would never dare cross again. But she just kept staring at him, those aquamarine eyes so wide and dark in the rosy tint of the lamplight, as if she was summoning up the courage to say something he wouldn't want to hear.

She cleared her throat. 'So are you against marriage generally?'

Kulal's mouth hardened. Too right he didn't want to hear it—the question he'd been asked a million times, usually by women on the make. One he always slapped down as coldly and as finally as possible. But Hannah was not one of those women; she was his wife. She had succeeded where so many had failed and he couldn't slap her down, not completely.

'A man in my position is always expected to marry,' he said. 'But I saw no urgency to do so. For someone who doesn't believe in love, it was always going to be an academic exercise of settling down to produce a family at the optimum time.'

'And what would you consider to be the *optimum time*?' she echoed cautiously.

'Never?' he questioned sarcastically.

'Kulal, I'm serious.'

He shrugged. 'In perhaps a decade and a half, when I had reached fifty years and sown every last wild oat.'

'So this early and unwanted marriage has prevented you from having hundreds of different relationships? All those wild oats which will remain unsown.'

'I am not totally indiscriminate, Hannah,' he said gravely.

'But all that…all that unexplored opportunity,' she breathed. 'Won't it make you resentful?'

Kulal frowned, feeling momentarily wrong-footed. Surely *she* was the one who was supposed to be feeling resentful—not turning it around so that she was coolly interrogating *him*. 'I have no intention of straying, if that's what you're getting at. Infidelity is something I am vehemently opposed to—despite many of my royal peers feeling it their right to keep a mistress.'

He saw the surprise on her face as she brushed a heavy swathe of hair away from her forehead and blinked at him.

'I have the feeling I shouldn't be grateful just because you've told me you won't break our wedding vows, but the fact is that I am,' she said. 'And a little curious, too.'

Her instinctive intelligence was enough to make him prolong the conversation, even though he sensed he was venturing onto precarious territory. 'About what in particular?' he questioned.

'Well, you've told me you don't want love.'

'I don't.'

The rumpled white sheet barely covered the creamy swell of her breasts and her eyes suddenly seemed very bright. 'So why would you care about breaking your wedding vows, if another woman should suddenly take your fancy?'

He was on the verge of telling her that she looked so entrancing at that moment, that he couldn't imagine another woman holding a flame to her.

Until he remembered.

He tried not to remember, but sometimes it came out of nowhere and hit you like a vicious blow. He felt the pain course through him like a black tide and his body tensed. 'If you had grown up with parents like mine,' he said, a trace of savage bitterness creeping into his voice, 'you would understand.'

There was a pause before she spoke. 'But how can I understand if you won't tell me, Kulal?' she whispered. 'And if I understood, then maybe I could help you. Maybe you've forgotten that I grew up in a dysfunctional foster home which wasn't in any way loving, so I don't think anything you can tell me would shock me.'

He could see the eagerness on her face—a desire to help, which tugged at something deep inside him, but successfully he pushed the feeling away. Did she think it was that simple? That telling her would free him from the demons which had lived in his heart for so long? From his secret torture and sense of powerlessness? He felt a new resolve creep through his veins, for he would not give her that power. He would not give it to anyone. Hadn't he promised his brother that?

'And besides—' her voice had softened hopefully as she fixed him with that same wide-eyed stare '—we're married now. Aren't we supposed to share those kinds of things?'

There was a split-second pause before Kulal was galvanised into action. 'No, we're not,' he grated as he pushed the sheets from his naked body. 'I don't want that kind of marriage. I told you that from the start. Weren't you listening, Hannah? Or did you think you could change my mind just as soon as my ring was on your finger? Did you believe, as so many women mistakenly do, that it was just a matter of time and proximity before you could get me to backtrack on my words? In which case, I fear you may be a little premature, as well as misguided.' His voice hardened even more. 'In my culture, we don't spill out our innermost thoughts and feelings, as if life was just one long therapy session!'

'I didn't mean to pry,' she said, in a small voice. 'I was just trying to…help.'

'Well, don't because it's a waste of time—yours *and* mine. The past is none of your business, Hannah. You'd better accept that now or this isn't going to work. I will give you my fidelity and my support for our child. And I am prepared to make this marriage work within the framework we've laid out.'

'*You've* laid out, you mean.'

He shrugged. 'I'm the King. Sorry, but that's the way it works around here. I am not an unreasonable man and anything you require will be yours, within reason. But please don't ever ask me that again.'

There was a silence as she studied him, like someone hoping for a sudden miraculous change of heart, and Kulal saw the exact moment when resignation entered her eyes. When she realised that he meant every word he said.

'And that's the end of the discussion, is it?' she questioned flatly.

He nodded as he slid from the bed. 'Yes. And now I think it's time you got some sleep.'

'But…' She sat up and the white sheet fell to her waist, showing the luscious thrust of her breasts. 'Where are you going?'

He saw the alarm in her eyes, but years of practice meant he was able to steel his heart against it, even though he wasn't managing to remain quite so indifferent to the sight of her rose-pink nipples. Did she really think he was going to lie there night after night, while she fired her questions at him, shattering those sleepy moments of post-coital intimacy and ruining them? Should he tell her the reasons why he didn't want love and why he never would?

No.

Not on their wedding night. His mouth hardened. Perhaps not ever.

'I'm going to sleep next door. It's better that way.'

'Better?'

'Once again, I will draw your attention to royal protocol,' he said softly. 'It is quite normal for the

Sheikh and his Sheikha to sleep separately—a pattern which was set many centuries ago. We can still be intimate.' He reached for his discarded robe. 'But you need your rest, Hannah. And I'm going to make sure you get it.'

CHAPTER TEN

THERE WERE TWO different ways of dealing with a problem. Hannah knew that better than anyone. Stepping from her bath, she bent forwards a little as the servant wrapped a fluffy towel around her damp shoulders. You could either accept the problem and learn to live with it, or you could try to solve it. And hadn't she spent her life trying to do the latter?

She watched rose petals swirling round and round as water drained away from the golden bathtub. When she and Tamsyn had been hungry as children, she'd found food, hadn't she? And when her schooling had suffered as a result of her having to keep house, she'd tried to teach herself. Even when her lack of formal qualifications had led to what some people might have considered the non-aspirational job of chambermaid, she had worked hard and earned herself promotions. Necessity had made her one of life's fixers and that was the way she operated.

So couldn't she apply the same criteria to her marriage—to find a way to elevate it from its current state of stalemate? To make it into something more meaningful, despite Kulal's determination that it should exist only on the most superficial of levels? She swallowed. Because she was finding that what she had was not enough.

Not nearly enough.

She had a husband who was physically present but emotionally distant. A man who occupied himself by day—and sometimes evenings, too—with the many demands placed on him. Oh, occasionally he made a space for her in his diary, when for a brief time she felt as if she was actually sharing his life rather than living on the periphery of it. Times when she would accompany him to a state banquet, or the opening of some new medical centre, or perhaps they would eat dinner together—but that was the exception, rather than the rule. The only time she really had Kulal to herself was in bed at night.

Patting her skin dry, she sighed, because that wasn't quite true. Even being in bed with him was time-limited. Once they had satisfied their mutual desire several times over, he would slip away to sleep in his own room, rising at five to saddle his horse and pound the desert sands until his hard body was sheened with sweat and little tendrils of black hair clung to his face. She knew this because once, long after he'd left her bed, she'd heard a noise and, on getting up to investigate, had found him stripping off in one of the anterooms of their vast suite. He had pulled the damp shirt from his body and had been in the process of unzipping his jodhpurs when Hannah had walked in and he had frozen.

So had she. Because the sight of Kulal undressing was overwhelming enough to make her heart race erratically. Oh, she got to see his naked body at night—every night, as it happened—but at times that felt almost stage-managed and this totally unexpected half-clothed version of him was unbelievably erotic. She hadn't meant to be provocative when her tongue had slid out to slowly moisten her lips, but the increased tension in Kulal's muscular torso had suggested that he'd found it so.

As she stood in her long, diaphanous nightgown, her rounded shape must have been very apparent with the lamplight shining through the folds of silk-chiffon, and she'd seen her husband's black eyes roving greedily over her body before he deliberately lifted his gaze to hers.

'You are not ill?' he demanded.

She'd shaken her head. 'I heard a noise, that's all. It woke me up.'

He'd lifted his broad shoulders in apology, pointing to the discarded riding crop which had lain beside one leather-booted foot, which had been tapping at the marble floor with impatience. 'I must have thrown that down with more force than I intended.'

She'd wanted to ask him why. Just as she'd wanted to ask him whether he might break his cast-iron rule and take her into his arms and kiss her. Now. Here. No matter how damp and sweaty he was. She had held her breath for one long moment when such a scenario had seemed possible—if the darkening of his eyes and the hungry hardening of his lips had been anything to go by—before he'd given her a dismissive smile.

'Forgive me for waking you.'

'I don't mind.'

'You should. A pregnant woman needs her sleep.' There had been a pause. 'Go back to bed, Hannah.'

The memory retreated as Hannah bent down to dry her toes, then pulled a silky robe over her head. Was that what happened in relationships? Were you always seeking something more, no matter how much you had? And wasn't the danger that she could jeopardise what they *did* have, if she allowed these restless longings to take over?

So she tried to count her blessings and to pray that some of Kulal's icy reserve might melt a little. One morning, he had flown her to the north-eastern side of Zahristan, to his royal beach house, where they had sat beneath a shaded canopy and watched the glitter of the sun on the Murjaan Sea as they'd sipped fire-berry cordial. Their small contingent of protection officers had been entirely female, giving Hannah the opportunity to swim in the enormous pool which was surrounded by palm trees. The silken waters had rippled deliciously over her skin and she'd seen Kulal smile when she'd given a little squeal of delight.

'Come and join me?' she had questioned shyly.

Uncharacteristically, he had hesitated before telling her he needed to make a conference call to New York, and that brief pause had been enough to make a flicker of hope enter her body. Because in that moment, hadn't he been tempted by an intimacy which wasn't just about sex?

And the trouble with hope was that it was like a weed—it grew wildly with the slightest bit of encouragement. Hannah wondered if it was all in her imagination, or whether Kulal's nocturnal visits were getting longer. Last night, it had been almost dawn before he had left the rumpled sheets to retreat to his own bedroom. Her eyelids had fluttered briefly open as she had watched him dressing in the dim light, longing for the time when he might spend an entire night with her. But she didn't dare ask him outright. Not after the humiliation of their wedding night. Not when she suspected such an appeal would prompt the proud desert King into doing the very opposite.

In the meantime, her pregnancy was progressing with textbook perfection. Each day her bump grew bigger, ticking off every developmental milestone along the way. The palace doctor declared herself delighted with Hannah's progress during their regular consultations, though the Sheikh had been absent from all of these.

'It would be inappropriate for the King to be present during such an intimate examination,' Kulal had said in reply to her tentative query about whether he might one day accompany her.

It was an old-fashioned point of view, but in many ways he was an old-fashioned man despite his western business dealings and cosmopolitan lifestyle prior to his marriage. He didn't seem to mind that royal law decreed that the sex of their unborn child should be known only to the attending doctor, even though Hannah was longing to find out if she was having a boy or a girl. Sometimes she reflected on how different Zahristan was from the world she had grown up in.

But somehow, despite all the odds, she liked it and found a peace there she'd never known before. She liked the quiet and beauty of walking in the palace gardens, or drinking her tea in the vast courtyard, with its cobalt-blue mosaic floor and the mingled scent of orange blossom and gardenia filling the air. She liked it when she was appointed a female aide and two female protection officers so that she was able to explore the ancient museums and artefacts in the nearby city of Ashkhazar, though she preferred to make these visits unannounced, so that there wouldn't be too much fuss. And she loved the huge library in the palace itself because, for the first time in her life, she actually had the time and the opportunity to read.

It felt magical to have endless rows of beautifully bound leather books at her fingertips and she began to read up more about Zahristan history, partly because she wanted to take her role as Sheikha seriously and partly because she wanted to understand Kulal's land and, by definition, him. She read that he was from a long line of Zahristan kings from his father's side and that his mother had been a princess from the neighbouring land of Tardistan. But there seemed to be gaps in the various accounts of his family history, even in the more modern publications—and it was only on a neglected shelf in a hidden alcove that she discovered a short biography about Kulal himself.

Her eyes scanned the pages eagerly, her eyes drinking in the portraits of his hawk-like features and flashing black eyes. There were descriptions of his exemplary school record and his daring exploits when he'd run away as a teenager to fight in the fierce border battle with Quzabar. There was an account of his father's lying-in-state and the political turmoil before Kulal's subsequent accession to the throne, but practically nothing about his mother's early death, other than the fact it was 'tragic'. And if Kulal was the younger of twin brothers, as was stated, it didn't explain why he had taken the throne instead of his older brother, Haydar. Hannah wanted to know, but instinct told her not to pry. That the answers she sought would only come about if she and Kulal grew closer as a couple—and wasn't she attempting to help that process along, by increasing the amount of time they spent together?

She'd quickly realised that Kulal working late into the evening before he came to bed was an evasive tactic. She realised that he preferred her to be waiting and ready for sex—she guessed because that ruled out the need for conversation other than the 'do you like it when I do that?' variety. She remembered those far-away days when she'd cleaned his suite in Sardinia when they used to chat about *stuff.* When once in a while he'd even teased her. Couldn't they get back to easy conversations like that—and the sort of intimacy which didn't involve her gasping out her pleasure as he drove into her eager body?

She told herself that the only reason she'd decided to start waiting until Kulal returned to their suite before retiring for the night was so they could chat. But deep down she knew that wasn't the whole truth. Deep down she realised she had started to care for her husband in a way he had emphatically warned her against. A way which felt frighteningly close to love, even though she told herself that wasn't possible.

But something had changed.

She wasn't sure how or when it had happened, because it wasn't the obvious things which had made her feel so differently about him. Not the muscular body which transported her to heaven and back every night. Or the ruler in all his finery with people bowing before him. It was the man with the occasional flicker of vulnerability in his eyes before the shutters came crashing down—that was the Kulal who had captured Hannah's imagination and then her heart. Was it so wrong to wonder if she could ever forge a tiny place for herself in *his* heart?

Her silken robes whispered as she walked over to the desk where she'd left her book open and the dull thud of the outer doors of their suite told her that Kulal had returned. Instantly, she felt her heart begin to thunder.

'Hannah?'

The sound of his voice was enough to send desire rippling down her spine and Hannah struggled to keep the hungry tremble from her voice. 'I'm in here!'

He walked into the bedroom, appearing startled to see her sitting at the desk, a halo of golden lamplight surrounding her. 'You're not in bed?' he questioned.

'As you see,' she said, with a smile. 'I thought I'd wait for you and do a spot of reading.' She put a bookmark in her book and closed it. 'How did your meeting with the Sultan of Marazad go?'

Kulal felt momentarily disorientated because he hadn't been expecting to see her waiting up for him. He swallowed. The sight of her alluring body was making him want to ravish her with a hunger which never seemed to wane, no matter how many times he took his fill of her. And it had never happened to him before—not like this. Every night since their wedding had been spent in her arms and not once had he grown bored. Unusually, he'd found himself cancelling trips to Europe and the States—feeling it wasn't really fair to abandon his pregnant wife in a strange new country, even though no such complaint had come from her. Despite the huge leap of being catapulted from chambermaid to queen, she hadn't been in the least bit clingy or dependent. She had been…

He swallowed.

She had been irresistible.

Beguiling him little by little—her shy sexual confidence had increased daily until he wondered which of them was the tutor and which the pupil. But it wasn't just sex she excelled at. It was other stuff, too. She seemed to instantly grasp what was important to him and what was not. She didn't say unnecessary things or do that glazed-eye thing women did when they were *pretending* to be interested in your job. Her interest in his work seemed genuine. His gaze distracted by the hard points of her nipples, which were thrusting against her pink gown, he dragged his mind back to the question she'd just asked him. Something about a meeting…

'It was good,' he said vaguely, even though this particular meeting had been months in the planning. 'Malik was unusually compliant.'

'So you think he's eager to embrace solar power at last?'

Kulal frowned. He didn't remember discussing that either, but he supposed he must have done. And why the hell was he getting into a discussion about renewable energy when he'd come here specifically to make love to her? 'Not nearly as eager as I am to embrace *you*,' he murmured, walking over to the desk and switching off the lamp, before pulling her to her feet. 'You should be in bed.'

Those amazing eyes widened. 'I've been reading.'

'It's late.'

'So what? I'm pregnant, Kulal—and I'm getting plenty of sleep. The doctor says I'm in peak health and right now I feel wide awake.'

'That's good. Because so do I.' He slid his hand

down over one undulating hip and instantly heard a long breath escape from her lips.

'Kulal.' He heard her swallow. 'I… I wanted to ask you some more about the solar power initiative and…and…*oh*!'

Her words faded away as his lips brushed hungrily over her neck. 'Which is the very last thing I want to talk about, Hannah. I'd rather concentrate on…*this*…' He started rucking up the gauzy gown to explore the silken territory of her thighs, his fingers finding her moist heat as he explored further. 'Wouldn't you?' he said unsteadily.

'Well…' She tipped her head to one side as if she was giving the question careful consideration, but he saw her eyes become opaque as his finger found her sweet spot and began to drum softly against it.

'You were saying?' he prompted softly.

'I don't…remember,' she moaned.

And neither did he. She felt so good and tasted so good that he could wait no longer. With a low groan, he picked her up and carried her over to the bed, ignoring her habitual protestations, because although she was almost six months pregnant with his child, he could still lift her with ease. She was wearing her nightgown, but Kulal was too hungry to care. In fact, he couldn't even wait to remove his own robes. But silk and satin could be pushed aside enough for him to gain all the access he needed and before too long she was breathlessly urging him to enter her. Kulal needed no second bidding as he filled her with an erection that had never felt quite so hard. Each thrust seemed to take him deeper. He felt as if he wanted to explode. As if nothing else in the world existed outside this room and this bed. He teetered on the brink of pleasure until at last she gave a strangled cry and almost immediately he let go with a harsh and breathless shout of his own.

Kulal didn't know how long he lay there before withdrawing from her, but her face was flushed and her eyes dark as they gazed at each other in the lamplight. 'That was a very welcome homecoming,' he said eventually.

'I'm glad,' she said demurely.

'Where the hell did you learn to be so...*respon-*

sive?' He gave a wry smile. 'Or are you just one of life's natural seductresses?'

'I've read some stuff,' she admitted a little shyly. 'I figured that an inexperienced wife might drive you into the arms of someone else if I wasn't careful.'

The unexpected candour and humility of her response made Kulal's heart punch painfully in his chest. 'But I promised you my fidelity,' he growled.

'I know you did, but I…'

She seemed about to say something else when he saw a shadow cross over her face, and instead she shrugged.

'What?' he probed.

'It doesn't matter. Honestly.' She fastened her arms around his neck and planted a lingering kiss on his lips. 'What matters is that you should enjoy your coming home at night as much as I do.'

'I certainly enjoy coming,' he mused.

'Kulal!'

He gave a low laugh. 'I don't really think you're in any position to be shocked by my words, Hannah—not when you seem pretty unshocked by some of the things we do together. Now…' his voice dipped '…why don't we rid you of this nightgown—beautiful as it is—which, in my haste to be inside you, I neglected to remove?'

He helped her slide out of her nightdress, but took his time while undressing himself, deliberately making himself step back from the easy intimacy which seemed to have developed between them. Because sometimes, didn't disquiet whisper over his skin—as warm and as insidious as the slow trickle of blood? Instinctively, his fingertips went to the ridged scar which ran all the way from nipple to belly. At the time, he hadn't felt the knife enter his body because he had been on a rush of adrenalin, and sometimes he felt the same way now, when he was in bed with his wife.

He had warned Hannah what he would and wouldn't tolerate within their marriage yet he hadn't expected her to be quite so *accepting* of his demands. Hadn't he anticipated rebellion once she realised he would not bend the stringent rules he had imposed on their union? But she had confounded all his expectations. She hadn't sulked, or bargained, or pleaded for him to spend the whole night with her. She hadn't drummed her fingernails on the table and told him what *she* wanted. She had just seemed to slot into palace life as if she'd been born to it. According to his aides, she spent her days quietly, either in the gardens or in the library, with the occasional trip into the city as she prepared for the birth of their child.

'Kulal.' Her voice sounded soft—like a harp playing on a spring evening.

'What is it?' Yanking off his robe, he slid into bed beside her.

'I want…'

'What do you want, Hannah?' he questioned indulgently.

'To…to kiss you.'

It was such an innocent request—how could he refuse? Why would he even *want* to refuse? Was it because he detected a trace of some indefinable emotion in the melodic caress of her words? Or because kissing represented an intimacy which sometimes felt as if it was mushrooming out of his control? As he bent to brush his lips over hers, he told himself it was only a kiss, but within seconds they were having sex again. If she hadn't been pregnant he might have been a little rougher with her—made her ride him like a cowboy riding a bucking bronco, to demonstrate that this was nothing more than physical.

But if she hadn't been pregnant, she wouldn't be here, he reminded himself as his orgasm hit him like a muffled burst of stars. And that was his last coherent thought before he fell into a deep sleep.

His dreams were fitful and he awoke to an unfamiliar smell, forcing open his eyelids to see Hannah on the other side of the bedroom, tipping strong coffee into two tiny glimmering cups. Sitting up in bed, he raked his fingers back through his tousled hair—scowling in confusion as he noticed slats of bright sunlight slanting through the shutters.

'What time is it?' he demanded.

She was undulating towards him, her silken gown flowing around her like a waterfall as she carried one of the tiny golden cups.

'Almost nine,' she replied, putting the coffee down beside him. 'You slept right through.'

Was he imagining the hint of triumph in her voice and the look of satisfaction on her face?

'Why didn't you wake me?' he questioned, pushing aside the sex-scented sheets and watching her aquamarine gaze automatically flicker towards the hardness at his groin, before she lifted her eyes to his face. 'You know I like to exercise my stallion before dawn.'

'I know you do. But you looked so peaceful lying there that I couldn't bring myself to wake you. And I assumed one of the servants would take your horse out in your absence.'

His mouth thinned. 'How quickly you have become used to having servants, Hannah,' he commented drily. 'But I think we're both aware that nobody gives Baasif a ride quite as hard as I do.'

He saw colour creep into her skin and knew that she wasn't thinking about horse-riding. The throb at his groin intensified. Neither was he. But she needed to understand that this wasn't going to become like a regular marriage, with them spending every constricting moment in each other's company. Did she think he would give up his morning ride and become sedentary and fat? To lie in bed with her, drinking coffee and eating pastries? He scowled as he reached for his robe.

'Why don't you drink your coffee, Kulal?' she said calmly and her words suddenly felt like the domestic kiss of death.

'I don't want any coffee,' he snarled.

He pulled the garment over his head and saw the disappointment on her face. But he would be tolerant with her. He wouldn't berate her for forcing him into something he had told her he didn't want—not when it was his own fault for falling asleep like that. But it would not happen again, he thought grimly. Never again would he waken to some commonplace scene of domesticity, with her giving him that doe-eyed look which was suddenly making him feel so *trapped*.

He thought she might be about to do the sensible thing and just let him leave, but she didn't. She crossed the room and stood in front of him, reaching up to cup his jaw and to run a questing thumb over it—as if testing for herself how rough his new growth of beard was first thing in the morning. It was as much as Kulal could do not to flinch, but somehow he stopped himself in time. And then she started to speak.

'Kulal?'

He stepped away from her touch. 'I hope this is urgent, Hannah,' he said warningly.

She drew in a deep breath as if she hadn't heard him. 'Must you leave my bed every night, as though I am your mistress instead of your wife?'

He raised his eyebrows, trying to keep it light. 'You don't think that such behaviour adds a piquant spice to our relationship?' he drawled.

'You're all the spice I need, Kulal,' she said almost shyly and then did something she hadn't done for many weeks.

She blushed.

She blushed and Kulal felt the whisper of danger.

'Haven't we already had this discussion?'

'Yes, but I wondered whether we might review things.'

'*Review* things?' he echoed. 'Like what?'

She shrugged. 'I like waking up beside you,' she said shyly. 'Just as I like you holding me tightly all night long.'

He frowned. 'Was I holding you all night long?'

'You don't remember? You certainly were. You were murmuring things to me in Zahristanian in the middle of the night.' She smiled, and the blush deepened. 'I didn't have a clue what the words meant, but they sounded…'

His head jerked up. 'Sounded *what*?'

Nervously, she ran the tip of her pink tongue in a moist and curving path over her lips as if she had suddenly recognised that this line of conversation was unwise. 'Nothing,' she said quickly.

But it was too late because just then, Kulal *did* remember. Something she'd whispered in his ear in the deepest point of the night when he was deep inside her.

Kulal, I love you.

Kulal, I love you so much.

Had that been her response to his own words of appreciation, which had probably been nothing more than murmured praise for her ability to make him orgasm so often? Had she misinterpreted them—seen her opportunity to strike, by professing for him what he had *emphatically told her he didn't want*? He felt the icy clench of rage around his heart as he studied her. Did she think everything had suddenly changed just because they were sexually compatible and could spend the occasional evening eating dinner without having a row? Did she think she could disregard his wishes in order to pursue her own? 'What's this all about, Hannah?' he questioned.

She paced around the suite a bit, moving her shoulders restlessly like someone eager to get a whole load of stuff off their chest. 'I've read various things about your childhood,' she said at last. 'Although the information available was quite patchy.'

'And?' he questioned, though she appeared not to notice the warning in his voice.

'And I can see you probably had to learn to be independent because your mother died when you were so young and your father was away a lot.

But I can understand that independence, because I had to grow up fast, too.'

'That's enough!'

'Please, Kulal.' Her words started to falter when she saw his expression, but she forged on. 'Let me just say this.'

'I would strongly advise against saying anything else, since I need to shower and get dressed and go to see my advisors,' he said, but she carried on as if he hadn't spoken and fleetingly Kulal thought how audacious it was that the one-time chambermaid should so openly disregard the wishes of the King.

'I'm not asking for the impossible,' she said, still in that same soft voice. 'Just that you relax and let what happens happen. That you stop leaving my bed straight after we've had sex.' She cleared her throat and slanted him a hopeful smile. 'I've never seen you looking so contented as when you were asleep this morning.'

It might have worked if he hadn't remembered her words and Kulal realised it would be easier to pretend he hadn't heard them. But he knew women well and once that phrase was out there, she would say it again. Oh, it might not be for a week—maybe even a month—but there would be some vulnerable point when she mistook passion or kindness for something more. She would say them again and expect him to start saying them back. And that was never going to happen.

'Have you fallen in love with me, Hannah?' he questioned softly and as she drew in a sharp intake of breath, he could see the flicker of hope in her pale eyes.

'Yes,' she breathed. 'I've tried so hard not to but it's happened almost without me realising it. I love you, Kulal. I love you so much.'

Kulal stared at the woman before him, her eyes bright with passion and her cheeks flushed with emotion.

His wife.

His wife who had just told him she loved him.

His lips curved as he felt anger course through his veins. 'What do you want me to say, Hannah?' he snarled. 'That I love you, too? Because, believe me—that is never going to happen.'

CHAPTER ELEVEN

HANNAH MET KULAL'S icy gaze and desperately wished she could rewind the clock. To take back the words which had stumbled out of her mouth almost before she'd realised she was saying them. Why on earth had she done that? Indulged herself with a declaration of love when she knew for a fact that Kulal didn't want it?

Because she had been unable to hold it back any longer. She'd blurted it out last night when he'd been making love to her and that was almost understandable, because she had been in the middle of an orgasm at the time. But there had been no such excuse just a few moments ago, had there? Yet she had been unable to hold it back any longer. It had been like a dam building up inside her, before bursting free and washing away all reservations in its path.

'My words were unconditional, Kulal,' she amended quickly. 'I wasn't expecting anything in return. Honestly. We can just carry on like before and forget I ever said it.'

Kulal shook his head, his cynicism obvious from the hardening of his lips. 'But life isn't like that, Hannah. You must realise that. You've changed everything. It can't possibly go back to how it was before. How could it? Our relationship will grow increasingly one-sided and you'll want more.' He paused. 'More than I can ever give you.'

'Kulal—'

'No!' The word shot from his lips as he glared at her. 'Perhaps it's time you heard the whole story and then you might understand. Do you want to know why the information about my childhood is so "patchy", Hannah? Do you?'

Something in his tone was frightening her. Warning her that she might have done something from which there was no coming back. Hannah clenched her fists. 'Not…not if you don't want to tell me.'

'Of course I don't want to tell you! I'd rather not have to think of it even at the end of my days,' he iced out. 'But you've forced me into a corner, haven't you? Because that's what women do best. They push and push until there's nowhere left to go.' His face grew dark, almost savage. 'So maybe it's time you heard the facts about my childhood.'

Hannah forced herself to sit down on one of the chairs, but its soft seat did little to ease her rigid posture as she folded her hands in her lap and looked at him. 'Okay,' she breathed.

There was silence for a few seconds, a silence so profound that she wondered if he'd changed his mind and didn't part of her wish he had? But then he began to speak and his voice was as cold as a winter wind whistling through the rooms of an empty house.

'It was a match like so many royal marriages in this region,' he said. 'A traditional marriage intended to unify two great dynasties from neighbouring countries. After the birth of his sons, my father kept mistresses, but he was always discreet about them. And yes, you can widen your eyes in horror, but that was the way things were in those days, Hannah. Once more, I ask you to look no further than your own royal family to see that kings and princes have always broken the fundamental rules of relationships. The difference was that my mother refused to accept it. She didn't want that kind of marriage. She wanted a modern *romantic* marriage—and that had never been on the cards.'

'So what…happened?' she questioned as a long silence followed this pronouncement.

His mouth twisted. 'The love she professed to feel for him became an obsession. She tried everything in her power to command his attention. She was his constant shadow. Wherever he turned, she was there. I remember she used to spend hours in front of the mirror, refining and redefining her appearance to try to become the woman she thought he wanted. Once, she even sought out one of his mistresses and attacked her—flaying her fingernails down the woman's face. It took a lot of money to hush that up.' He his face grew even darker as he continued. 'And the irony was that, not only was her neediness driving my father further away, it blinded her to everything else around her. In the midst of her quest to win his heart, she neglected the needs of her young family.'

'You mean you?'

He nodded. 'Yes, me, but especially my twin brother, Haydar. I had run away to fight in the border battles with Quzabar—I think I used the war as an excuse to escape from the toxic atmosphere within the palace.' His voice grew bitter. 'Now I berate myself for my cowardice.'

'Cowardice?' she echoed. 'A teenager who was honoured for his bravery during that war? Whose body is still scarred from the aftermath?'

'Yes,' he hissed. 'Because Haydar was still here. He was the one who bore the brunt of her increasingly bizarre behaviour.'

'She sounds like she was depressed.'

'Of course she was depressed!'

As his words faded away, Hannah took the opportunity to ask another question. 'And did she ever…did she ever see a doctor?'

'Yes.' Distractedly, he began to pace around the vast room, but when he stopped and turned back to face her, a terrible look had distorted his features into a bleak mask. 'But people can only be helped if they want to be helped, and she didn't.'

'So what happened?' she whispered.

He picked up a small box inlaid with jewels as if to study it, but Hannah suspected he didn't really see it. Putting it carefully back down on the gilded table, he looked up. 'It's not uncommon for families to normalise bizarre behaviour and that's exactly what we did. Everyone lived with it the best they could, and time passed. I only heard second-hand what happened next. Things had been bad. Worse than usual. She refused to leave her room, no matter what the inducement. By this stage, my father had renounced all his other women and was trying to make amends, but it was too late. Haydar went to show her a piece of wood he'd carved for her in the shape of one of the rainbow birds which fly in the palace gardens and that's when he found her…'

His voice had faltered, its grim tone warning Hannah that something unspeakable must have happened. 'Kulal?' she said softly.

'She was dead.'

Hannah saw the blanching of his olive skin and wondered if perhaps she'd asked enough questions but by now she couldn't stop. Because didn't she get the feeling that Kulal had spent his whole life bottling this stuff up, so that it had fermented inside him like a slow poison? Couldn't this disclosure—no matter how painful—help liberate him from some of those locked-away demons, even if it darkened their own relationship as a result? 'How did she die?' she questioned clearly.

His eyes were bleak as they met hers. They looked empty. As if all the light had left them, never to return. 'She slashed her wrists,' he said eventually, not pausing when he heard Hannah's shocked cry, emotion shaking his voice so that it sounded like rock shattering. 'Then daubed our father's name in blood on the walls. And that was how Haydar found her.'

A terrible silence descended on them. Hannah slapped her fingers over her trembling lips and it was minutes before she could bring herself to respond. 'Oh, Kulal,' she whispered. 'I'm so sorry.'

'Of course you're sorry,' he iced back. 'We were all sorry. My father went half mad with guilt, and it nearly broke my brother. It's what made him leave Zahristan as soon as he reached eighteen. Why he renounced the throne so that I was forced to take his place as monarch, even though I am the younger twin and never wanted to rule. Why he has never returned to this country for almost seventeen years,' he finished bitterly. 'That's why the information about my mother's death is so *patchy*, as you defined it—because somehow, I'm still not sure how, the palace managed to hush it all up. But press coverage was also very different at that time. We had more control over the media. Now do you understand what made me the man I am, Hannah?'

She was nodding her head. 'Y-yes,' she said, trying to stop her voice from trembling.

'Why I have no desire for the demands of love?' he continued, still in that same harsh tone. 'It's a word I equate with selfishness and ego. A word which often contradicts itself because people use it as a justification for behaviour which is in no way *loving*. Now, if you can accept that, then maybe we can continue as we are. If you can accept that I can never give you love and that I have no desire to be loved by you, then I am prepared to make the best of this marriage of ours.' He paused and, briefly, his mouth softened. 'A marriage which has been surprisingly tolerable, given its mismatched nature.'

Hannah told herself he wasn't trying to be insulting as she absorbed his words. 'And if I can't?'

He met her eyes, all that softness having left lips which were now hard and unsmiling. 'Then we're in trouble.'

Hannah thought they were in trouble now. Deep trouble. Her instinct after hearing such a terrible story would have been to have taken her husband in her arms and held him close. To have stroked the raven darkness of his hair with fingers intended to comfort, because comfort was something she was good at—she'd comforted Tamsyn time and time again when her little sister had sobbed into her neck during their neglected childhood. But Kulal mistrusted closeness. He didn't want affection unless it involved sex—and suddenly Hannah realised that his revelation had the power to change everything. Would it make her feel ridiculously self-conscious around him? If she was extra-tender towards him in bed would he think she was developing a love for him which might one day border on the obsessive, like his mother's? Was she going to have to walk on eggshells whenever she was in his company, terrified he would misinterpret the simplest of gestures? And all that in addition to being in the inevitable spotlight of royal life…

Could she bear it?

Turning away from him, she walked over to the shutters, pulling them open to let in the bright light which flooded into the room. It should have been a symbolic lightening, but the atmosphere remained dark and heavy as Hannah stared outside. Their bedroom overlooked the rose garden, where a beautiful fountain was sending sprays of water arcing through the air in a shimmer of rainbows, but today the simple beauty of the scene made her feel unbearably sad. Often she would sit in the shade of the veranda outside, just enjoying her book in the peace of the afternoon. But somehow she could never imagine doing that again, because her newfound knowledge had changed everything. Her eyes had been opened and she could no longer pretend.

And that was the problem. Before, she could allow herself to daydream about her husband and hope they would get closer. Actually, what she'd secretly wanted was for them to fall in love. But that was never going to happen. Kulal would never *allow* it to happen—but at least now he'd given her a reason. Why *wouldn't* he run screaming from love, when his mother hadn't shown him or his brother any? When she'd made a mockery of the word by sacrificing herself on the altar of her broken dreams.

'I don't know,' she said huskily and saw his black eyes narrow. 'I don't know whether I can live like that, Kulal.'

He inclined his head. 'Thank you for your honesty, at least.'

'And if I can't, what then?'

His frown deepened as her words tailed off. 'You'll have to be a little more specific than that.'

She supposed she should be grateful that they were discussing the flaws in their marriage so openly, but it was cold comfort indeed. She looked him straight in the eyes and dared voice the fear which had been nagging at her from the very start. 'If I decided I couldn't endure this life, would you try to stop me from bringing up our baby as a single mother?'

Clenching and unclenching fists hidden by the silken folds of his robes, Kulal glowered. If she'd asked him this question even a few weeks ago, the answer would have been an emphatic yes. He would have told her that such a proposition was out of the question. He would have used his wealth and his power to cut Hannah out of their child's life as much as possible. To sideline her and ensure their baby could be brought up as a Zahristan citizen, rather than as a westerner. But that was before he had grown to know her better. Before he'd realised that the pain of her own past had made her into the person she was. She would be a good mother, he recognised instinctively, and it would be wrong to wrench her from her child.

Yet the alternative was something he couldn't bear to contemplate. Surely she didn't imagine he would allow her to bring his son or daughter up in England, thus denying his child its royal roots and all that went with that?

'I don't know,' he said savagely, which was as close to the truth as he dared go. 'Obviously, the best solution would be for you to remain here. I have pledged to you my fidelity and now you will understand why I would never go back on that promise. If you can settle for friendship and respect, as well as the rare chemistry which exists between us—I think we could have a very satisfactory life together.'

He wasn't offering the moon and the stars, but at least he was being honest—and couldn't that be enough? Hannah licked her lips. She didn't know. But if she couldn't accept the limitations of their relationship, then she was going to be very unhappy. And she couldn't afford to be unhappy. Not for their baby's sake. Not for Kulal's, either. How could she bear to put him through any more pain when he'd already suffered so much already? The unwilling King who had made a success of the role which had been forced upon him.

But making promises she might not be able to keep was dangerous and what he was asking was too important to fire off an answer without thinking it through. Even though she had told him her love was unconditional and she wanted nothing in return, what if she couldn't stick to that? What if she found herself yearning for more than Kulal was ever capable of giving her? Wouldn't that drive a terrible wedge between them?

'I don't know,' she said. 'I… I need time to think.'

'How much time?'

She met his searing black gaze and for the first time since she'd known him, Hannah felt like his equal. It was as if all that had happened had given her the strength to finally shake off the insecurities which had helped define her for so long. Proudly, she tilted her chin. 'As long as it takes.'

He shook his head. 'That's not good enough, Hannah,' he clipped out. 'You're pregnant. We need some sort of timescale.'

'Is a week reasonable?'

'That depends,' he growled. 'You must know that I'm reluctant to let you return to England.'

'Scared I won't come back?'

'You think I'd let you run away?' he challenged softly.

But the crazy thing was that Hannah had no desire to go back home to work this out. It wasn't as if she had any sanctuary there—just a stubborn little sister who seemed to have slipped entirely off the radar since the night of the wedding. She didn't even have a home of her own any more. She didn't want England, with all its associations and familiarities, clogging up her head as she tried to work out what was best for everyone.

'No,' she said. 'I want peace and quiet. I'd like to go to your beach house.'

'On your own?'

'Isn't that the whole point?'

He looked at her for a long moment before he nodded. 'Very well,' he said, at last.

She supposed it was a victory of sorts but somehow it felt hollow. His words sounded so *distant* as they matched that cool new expression on his face. Almost as if he was already beginning to detach himself from her. As if he was practising for a different kind of ending. Maybe he would be the one to make the decision for both of them. What if time spent apart made him realise he didn't want a wife, after all? There was nothing to prevent him from using his mighty power to gain custody of their baby and returning to his life of a single man. Hannah bit her lip. And wouldn't she have facilitated that, with her insistence of demanding time away in order to think?

But it was too late to change her mind. Too late to do anything other than watch as Kulal headed towards the double doors, his lips unsmiling as he slammed his way out of the room without a backward glance.

CHAPTER TWELVE

IT WAS VERY peaceful by the Murjaan Sea. The sunlit air had an almost luminous quality about it and the sound of the waves lapping gently against the sandy shore was hypnotic. Each morning, Hannah pulled back the floaty white curtains and opened the shutters so that she could gaze out at the azure glitter of the water. And for a moment, she would just stand there, taking in the elemental beauty while breathing in the clean desert air.

Accompanied by a team of three female protection officers, a qualified midwife and doctor, Hannah had taken just two extra servants with her to the Sheikh's beachside retreat. Kulal had wanted to send a much bigger contingent of staff including a chef—but on this, Hannah had stood firm. She'd told him she didn't want all the accoutrements of the palace or to set up *court* there.

She wanted a place which felt as close to ordinary as possible. To be able to go around unbothered by protocol, without the weight of expectation. Because she hadn't come here to play at being queen. She was here to decide how she wanted to spend her future and the choice was stark.

To live with a man who could never love her.

Or merely to exist without him.

She tried to imagine what it would be like if she went back to England—yet already it was hard to remember her life there. It felt like a country she'd visited a long time ago which was slowly fading from her memory. Much more dominant was the vivid nature of this desert land, which she found herself embracing despite her worries about the future.

Each morning, she swam in the infinity pool and, during the cool of the evening, explored the sprawling tropical gardens which Kulal had created there. But Hannah couldn't shake off the feeling of being under some kind of giant microscope. Sometimes it felt almost as if she was being *watched*—even though her security detail kept a safe but respectful distance. She told herself that she was being paranoid. Because who on earth would be able to get through the fortress-like security which surrounded the Sheikh's sprawling estate?

Her mind was like a butterfly, unable to rest on anything for long. She kept thinking about Kulal's hawk-like features and fathomless black eyes. Eyes which could blaze with passion or harden with a flintiness which made them resemble stone. Which was kind of fitting when she forced herself to think how emotionally cold he was. But, always a stickler for fairness, Hannah forced herself to think about other sides of his character, too. His strength and his determination to do the right thing, even if it wasn't what he really wanted. His honesty—and his courage. Sometimes you just had to go with instinct, and something in her heart told her he would be a loving father even if he could never be a loving husband.

Was that enough?

Wouldn't it have to be enough?

And meanwhile, she was finding it difficult to sleep. Despite the cool sea breezes which blew through the palace every evening, Hannah tossed and turned as she lay in bed, missing her husband more than she had thought possible. Because it was at night-time that the memories became difficult to ignore. The way it felt when he took her in his arms and kissed her. The way she trembled when he was deep inside her. Sometimes she would press her hands to her breasts and wish they were Kulal's hands, before guiltily snatching them away.

On the fifth night, she awoke from a troubled dream in the early hours, sitting bolt upright in bed, her skin bathed in sweat. Running the back of her hand over her damp brow, she looked around, her heart thudding. She had left the shutters open and through the floaty white curtains she could see the almost imperceptible lightening of the dawn. Her breath caught in her throat as she thought she heard a faint sound, her narrowed eyes making out the dark shape of a shadow moving outside the window, but it was gone so quickly she was certain she had imagined it. Brushing a damp lock of hair away from her heated cheek, she returned to the constant soundtrack which was playing inside her head. Could she go back to how she'd been before and manage to *stop* loving Kulal, or was that too much to ask?

For the first time in her life, she had found a problem with no real solution and the frustration of realising this made it impossible for Hannah to get back to sleep. The minutes ticked by and in the end, she gave up and got out of bed, splashing her face with cool water and slipping on some clothes. Through the window, she could see dawn lightening the horizon with a soft blaze of colour and she felt the stir of an idea. Why not witness the sun rising over the desert and see for herself how that stark place came to life? Hadn't Kulal told her often enough it was the best time—the time when he loved to ride his stallion, the heavy pound of Baasif's hooves the only sound apart from the occasional hiss of a circling vulture?

Scribbling a hasty note saying where she was going, Hannah shoved it under the door of her security detail who were sleeping nearby, then tiptoed through the silence of the dawn palace. She felt a sense of freedom as she let herself out and began to walk towards the desert, a light sea breeze lifting her sticky hair from the back of her neck. The fireworks of first light were beginning to explode all around her, and the pink sky was shot with yellow and gold and vivid streaks of purple. It was so beautiful, she thought wistfully—and if she hadn't woken up, she might have missed it.

She was careful to take a straight line from the gardens and not to venture far, because only a fool would risk getting lost in such an inhospitable place as this. But maybe her head was too busy for her to pay proper attention, because after a little while Hannah realised she couldn't see the outline of the palace any more.

Her heart began to race.

Don't panic, she told herself calmly. All she needed do was to retrace her footsteps in the sand. She glanced at her watch and frowned. Surely she hadn't been out here *that* long? With a touch of urgency now quickening her walk, she began to follow the sandy imprints back the way she'd come. But maybe the sea breeze was stronger than she'd thought because after a while, the footsteps grew fainter before eventually disappearing. A coating of fine dust had covered her path, and it was as if she had never been there.

She blinked as she tried to remember the basic rules of survival, cursing herself when she realised that she hadn't even brought water with her.

Because she hadn't been planning to stay.

Her heart began to race. Weren't you supposed to stay still in circumstances like these? Weren't some people clever enough to be able to tell where they were by the movement of the sun? She looked up at the vast dome of the sky and wondered if she had imagined the dark circling of a vulture overhead. It was already getting warmer, but Hannah shivered because in that moment, she felt very small and very alone. She was just wondering what to do next when suddenly the silence was broken by the loud thunder of hooves and she looked up to see the growing shape of an approaching horseman. A huge black horse was pounding across the desert, clouds of dust billowing as it moved with the fluidity of black oil pouring across the sand towards her.

She recognised the rider instantly. How could she not? That proud posture and uncovered raven hair was too unique to belong to anyone else other than the Sheikh. But as the horse drew closer, with a slowing of hooves and a snorting of flared nostrils, the only thing Hannah could see was the naked fury on her husband's face. With a thunderous expression, he leapt from the saddle, his hands reaching out to grasp her wrists as if he was afraid she might suddenly fall to the ground. Narrowed ebony eyes searched her face as he levered her closer so that she could smell the sweat and sandalwood of his heated body.

'I hope by the rise of the desert moon that you are not hurt,' he gritted out.

She nodded, wondering if he could feel the wild race of her pulse beneath his fingers. 'I'm fine.'

'No. You are not fine,' he bit out. 'I'll tell you

exactly what you are. You're a fool, Hannah. What do you think you're doing?'

'I couldn't sleep. I thought I'd get up to watch the sunrise,' she said, aware of how lame it sounded.

'And where the hell were your security detail?' he demanded.

A little shamefacedly, Hannah shrugged. 'Last night, I told them I was going to have a lie-in and didn't want to be disturbed. I left them a note.'

He gave a long, low curse in his native tongue. 'So why were you wandering around the desert on your own?'

'I told you. I wanted to see the sunrise.'

'Don't you know how dangerous it can be out here?'

Shaking herself free from his grasp and whipping her mobile phone from one of the pockets hidden in her silken robe, she held it up so that the silvery rectangle flashed in the sunlight. 'I came prepared,' she said triumphantly. 'I brought my phone with me.'

His lip curled in derision. 'You think *that* could

save you from the strike of a rattlesnake or the sting of a scorpion?'

But suddenly, Hannah recognised from his anger that this wasn't about the natural dangers of the desert, but about something else. Her eyes narrowed as suspicion began to form and to grow inside her head until she could no longer contain it. And neither should she. Wasn't it time that she addressed the terrible question she suspected would always hover in the darkness of her husband's mind, if she chose to ignore it? 'Why, Kulal,' she questioned quietly, 'what did you think I was doing?'

Kulal saw from her look of comprehension that she had a very good idea what he was thinking, but he shook his head, unwilling to articulate the fears which had rushed through his veins like poison.

'Nothing,' he grated.

'What? It's not *nothing*, is it?' she said again.

And suddenly Kulal was aware that she was the one doing the accusing and her aquamarine eyes were flashing with unaccustomed fire as she continued.

'Did you think I couldn't cope with the insecure future you were offering me and had decided to take the easy way out?' she demanded. 'Did you think I was going to dramatically wander out into the desert and kill myself? Is that what you thought, Kulal?'

He flinched beneath the cruel clarity of her allegation, but he couldn't deny that it was rooted in truth. Distractedly, he shook his head. 'I didn't know what to think.'

'Oh, yes, you did,' she breathed. 'You thought the worst of me because that's what experience has taught you to do. But I am not your mother, Kulal—and I never will be. I would never harm myself, nor the child I carry—not in a million years. What in heaven's name do I have to do to convince you of that?' She sucked in a breath which was ragged and shook her head. 'I think you need to stop blaming your mother for what happened.' Her voice grew gentle. 'She wasn't bad, you know—she was ill. Very ill. And because it was a different time, things like that just got pushed into a corner. People never used to talk about mental health issues because they were seen as something shameful, but that would never happen now. Your mum would have got the treatment she needed.' She swallowed. 'And maybe she would be here now, awaiting the birth of her first grandchild.'

'Hannah—'

'No. I haven't finished, Kulal.' She shook her head and seemed to take a long time before whispering her next words. 'You have to forgive her. And then let her rest in peace. Because until you do that, you can never find your own peace.'

He looked into her eyes and for once, he didn't turn away from the raw emotion he could read in their aquamarine depths. He could see the pain and the consternation which had all but wiped out the hope which had once flickered there. And suddenly Kulal realised that, in trying to protect himself, he had risked everything. He had offered Hannah a life without feeling and without love. He had arrogantly expected her to accept the meagre crumbs of affection he was prepared to offer. More than that, he had regarded her with a suspicion which had no basis in fact.

Wouldn't any woman in her position decide that she wanted no more of him and his controlling nature?

Was it too late for him to make amends?

Suddenly, he reached out and lifted her up into the saddle, her bewilderment muffling her objections as he jumped up behind her, one hand lying protectively around her belly while the other gripped the reins as he eased the horse forward.

'Kulal!' She seemed to find her voice at last. 'What…what do you…?'

But her words were lost on the desert wind as Kulal began to canter forward with the skill of a man who had ridden from the moment he could walk. Through the silken folds of her robe, he could feel the warmth of her body and sometimes the breeze tantalised him with the occasional drift of her scented hair. His throat grew dry. He thought of how he'd felt during the last five days without her and suddenly Kulal *did* feel fear.

Fear that it might be too late.

Fear that he might have lost her because of his overarching arrogance and stubbornly black-and-white view of the world.

He felt her relax as the distinctive shape of a huge tent appeared and the horse's pace slowed to a halt. Jumping down, he lifted her carefully onto the sand, but her expression was belligerent and her eyes unforgiving as she looked at him.

'Where are we?' she questioned stonily.

'In a Bedouin tent. Not far from the palace.'

Her eyes narrowed. *'Why?'*

'Why don't you come inside so we can discuss this away from the heat of the rising sun?'

'Said the spider to the fly!'

'And where I can offer you some cool refreshment?'

Her eyes lit up at this, but her nod was grudging. 'Very well.'

She pushed aside the tent-flaps and went inside, but Kulal had to dip his head to follow her. He took his time pouring fire-berry cordial from the stone flask which had kept it cool, telling himself he wanted her to enjoy her first view of this traditional desert homestead, with its sumptuous hangings, fretwork lanterns and silken rugs. But he was also hoping that allowing a little time to elapse might cool her temper. Already he was justifying his behaviour inside his head—and surely if he started being more accommodating towards her from now on, that would be enough to make her contented?

He was quietly hopeful as he handed her the drink, but could instantly see that his assessment had been poor, because after she'd gulped down most of the liquid and thumped the silver goblet down on a low table, she straightened up to glare at him, her eyes flashing in a way he'd never seen before.

'How did you know where I'd be?' she demanded.

Kulal winced. So. There was to be no gratitude for his masterful rescue of the lost Queen! She'd gone straight for the jugular. 'I've been camped out here all week,' he admitted, and saw from the unrelenting look on her face that it was pointless to do anything other than admit the whole truth. 'I have servants staying in nearby tents who were assigned to keep a watch on you at the beach palace, both day and night. They reported to me on your movements at all times.'

She wrinkled her forehead. 'Could that explain why I thought I saw a shadow creeping past my window a few hours ago?'

'Yes.'

'But I have my own protection officers with me, Kulal.'

'I know you do.' He gave a heavy sigh. 'But these are nomadic men of the desert, who know this territory better than any other. They can see things which the ordinary protection team is capable of missing—even a highly trained security detail.'

Her hands flew to her cheeks and he could see all the colour leeching away from her skin. 'So you sent people to spy on me? Because you didn't trust me?'

'I prefer to think of it as protecting you. And in view of what happened, wasn't I right to do so?'

'Protecting your baby, you mean.'

'And you,' he said simply. 'Protecting you is paramount to me, Hannah, because I love you.'

She shook her head and quickly turned away, not answering him immediately, and when she did, her words sounded strained. 'Don't try to manipulate me with words you don't mean.'

'But I do mean them,' said Kulal as, for the first time in his life, he began to express emotions he'd never even dared to feel before. He had always associated emotion with pain and loss and he didn't ever want to have to live through that again. But he could see now that he had no choice. That if he wanted Hannah to stay, he was going to have to get her to believe that what he felt for her was real. Something so big and new that at first he hadn't even recognised it—and when at last he had, it had scared the hell out of him. 'I've never been so sure about anything. Which is that I love you, Hannah,' he repeated shakily. 'I love you so much.'

'Don't you dare lie to me!'

Nobody had ever said that to Kulal before and with good reason—a fondness for sometimes brutal candour was the more usual accusation thrown at him, particularly by women. But now wasn't the time for a proud defence of his reputation; now he needed the kind of persuasive rhetoric which normally came so easily to him. And never had it seemed quite so far away. 'I've never met a woman like you before.'

'Obviously that's not true either!' she said contemptuously. 'You've spent your life surrounded by servants—and that's all I am.'

He told himself she was lashing out because she was scared, too—because the alternative was too daunting to acknowledge. He swallowed. What if she really *did* feel contempt for him—the kind of contempt which had wiped away all the love she'd once declared?

'I'm not talking about your job. I'm talking about your heart—which is a very big heart. You are the most kind and caring woman I've ever met, Hannah—as well as the most thoughtful.'

'*Sensible*, you mean?' she questioned witheringly, still with her back to him.

He shook his head. 'Your qualities go way beyond that. You are loyal—something you demonstrated when you were determined that I should be the first to hear about impending fatherhood when you could have easily sold the story to the press.' He pulled in a deep breath. 'And you have other characteristics, too—and I'm not talking about your obvious attraction or the way I can't seem to keep my hands off you.'

'Kulal…' she said warningly.

'I've never talked to anyone the way I talk to you,' he continued. 'About mountains and spiders and—'

'Don't you dare try to smooth-talk me with sentimentality, Kulal Al Diya,' she said, her voice cracking a little.

'You did the best thing for our baby by agreeing to marry me and then you tried to be the best wife you possibly could,' he forged on. 'And I threw it all back in your face.'

'Well, yes,' she whispered, turning back to face

him, and he was startled by the bright glitter of unshed tears in her eyes. 'You did.'

'Everything you accused me of was correct, but the one accusation which will not stand is the strength of my feelings for you—and I guess that time is the only thing which will prove that. That is, if you give me the gift of time.' His gaze was very steady as he looked at her. 'Because I would like the chance to prove I can be the kind of husband you deserve. The kind of father I pray I can be. And the kind of lover who never stops making you sigh with pleasure. The chance to show you how very much I love you. Will you give me that chance, Hannah?'

For a moment, Hannah couldn't answer because the emotion which was catching in her throat didn't allow her to. She recognised that this was a moment of real power and she tried to think about all the conditions she could demand of him.

But if she turned it around and thought of this as equality rather than power, it meant that she must do this without condition. To take him at his word. She had to trust him. It was a risk, but one she had to take. Because without trust, you could have nothing. No love and no real future.

Her voice was wobbling and the tears she seemed to have been holding back for so long began to stream down her cheeks like rivers. But that didn't matter. Nothing mattered other than the sure-fire certainty which pumped through her veins as she went into his open arms. 'Yes,' she whispered simply, her voice a little faint as she pressed her lips against his own wet cheek. 'I will give you that chance because I love you, Kulal—and deep down I know I always will.'

EPILOGUE

'I CAN'T BELIEVE you didn't tell me.'

Kulal turned back from the balustrade, where he had been standing watching the fiery sun sink slowly into the Murjaan Sea—a stunning spectacle indeed, but one which did not come close to competing with his wife's natural beauty. He gazed at her in a moment of grateful contemplation. The rose-gold light gilded her hair and cast shadows which emphasised the soft delicacy of her features.

'Tell you what?' he said as he walked over to where Hannah sat on the swinging hammock she had installed on the veranda of their beachside palace. But Kulal already knew the answer to his own question and so did Hannah. Just as he knew she must have a special reason for asking it again, and now.

'That girls were not allowed by law to inherit the Zahristan crown. That in order to accede to the throne, the child must be a boy.'

He smiled as he sat down beside her, taking her hand in his and beginning to massage it. 'And would it have made a difference in your decision to marry me?' he mused. 'If you had known, would you have insisted on waiting until the birth to discover if we were having a boy or a girl?'

Deep in love, Hannah smiled back. 'Of course it wouldn't,' she said. 'But I thought that having an heir was the main reason you wanted me to be your bride.'

'So did I,' he admitted, lifting her hand to his lips and kissing each finger almost reflectively. 'But there was obviously something immensely powerful burning between us, which had been there from the start. I guess I was too much of an emotional coward to admit it at the time—even to myself.'

'Not any more, though?' she questioned, her eyes glinting with mischief.

He met her moonlit gaze and shook his head. 'No, Hannah. Not any more.'

'And you're sure you don't want to have any more children, my darling? To try for a boy? Because I am quite willing to do that.'

So *that* was the reason she had brought it up. Kulal shook his head. 'No, my love. Four children is quite enough.'

'But—'

'But, yes,' he insisted softly, drawing her closer. 'I'm blissfully happy with my four daughters. Fate has not given us a son and I accept that. I am not risking your life in pursuit of a crown.'

Wordlessly, Hannah nodded. It had been an eventful time since they had been married—three glorious years which had been filled with both joy and fear. But life was like that, she realised, and they had faced those fears together and shared their joy until their hearts had felt fit to burst. It had been after the birth of their first daughter that Kulal had told her only a boy child could inherit the Zahristanian throne. They had wanted more children anyway, but Hannah had conceived far more quickly than either of them had anticipated. The birth of girl triplets had thrilled them immeasurably, but Hannah had almost died during the delivery and Kulal had asked her very sternly that for their children's sake—and his—could they now call their family complete?

'But who will inherit the throne?' she'd asked, with the sincerity of someone who felt a deep and enduring loyalty towards their adopted homeland.

Kulal's response had been a shrug which had convinced Hannah that he really didn't care. 'It will pass down to my cousin,' he said. 'Who is a good man. That's if my brother doesn't produce an heir in the meantime, which seems unlikely.'

'You don't care that your offspring will miss out on their inheritance?'

And she had cried when Kulal had smiled and shaken his head. 'The only thing I care about is you and my family, my dearest love.'

Hannah had met Haydar at last. Her husband's non-identical twin had finally returned to Zahristan for the celebrations marking the birth of the triplets. He was a charismatic but very silent man, Hannah remembered thinking—with a stillness about him which reminded her of one of Kulal's desert falcons just before it took flight. She'd wanted to take him in her arms and give him a sisterly hug of welcome, but hadn't dared. She'd thought how closed-off he seemed and had wondered if introducing him to a lovely woman might break down some of that shuttered reserve. But she wouldn't dare do that either. Because you couldn't dictate to your siblings how they should live their lives. And what made her think she knew better than anyone else, when she'd made her own share of mistakes in the past?

She thought about her own sister. She'd stopped trying to run Tamsyn's life for her, too. Kulal had gently told her it really was time to let go and Hannah had listened, even if it had been hard to stand back and let the fiery little redhead blaze her own unpredictable path.

Possibly one of the biggest changes in her husband's life had been his change of attitude towards his mother's death. He'd told Hannah that he'd given her words a great deal of thought and realised she was right. He had given the *Ashkhazar Times* an exclusive interview, talking frankly about his mother's suicide for the first time and the need to be open about mental health issues. The piece had gone viral. International charities had applauded his honesty and his candour, and confronting the issue had somehow allowed Kulal to make his peace with it at last—just as Hannah had predicted.

Turning her head, Hannah saw that the Sheikh was watching her and her heart welled up with love. And longing.

'You were looking very wistful just then,' he observed softly.

'Was I? I was thinking about everything which had brought us to the point we're at now.'

'And your conclusion is?'

Luxuriously, Hannah stretched, and smiled. 'My conclusion is that I've never been so happy and I wouldn't want it any other way.' For a second, the smile left her lips as she contemplated an alternative existence. One which didn't involve the hawk-faced Sheikh who was at the blazing centre of their family life. Which didn't involve four demanding little girls and the charity work for orphans which gave her so much fulfilment, because it was important to give something back. Especially when you had been given so much yourself…

'Sometimes I have to pinch myself,' she admitted on a whisper. 'To convince myself I'm not dreaming.'

'Is that so? I can think of a far more gratifying way of reinforcing reality than pinching,' murmured Kulal, as he gathered her in his arms and brushed his lips over hers. 'Would this do it, do you think?'

'Oh, yes. I think so,' she said.

He kissed her for a long time as some of the heat left the evening air. He kissed her until she began to move restlessly in his arms and then he picked her up and carried her through to their bedroom as the sea breeze billowed the floaty white curtains. He carried on kissing her as, slowly, he undressed her and laid her down on the bed and told her again and again how much he loved her.

'And I love you, too, Kulal,' said Hannah shakily. 'So very much.'

And suddenly they were no longer a king and a queen. They were just a man and a woman making love and speaking love, as the silvery moon rose high over the desert sky.

* * * * *